MW00939464

TWELVE BLOCKS

Written by Jonathan K. Miller

Jonathan K. Miller

This book is a work of fiction.The characters, incidents and dialogue are drawn from the author's imagination and are not to be construed as real. Any resemblance to actual events or persons, living or dead, is entirely coincidental.

CONTENTS

Jonathan K. Miller

PROLOGUE

Dr. Frank Deneb, a renown archeologist, heads a team of scientists to research the most important archeological discovery in the history of mankind at the request of the President of the United States, Calvin Sinclair. Chemical testing has revealed that the facility is approximately 2 million years old. As research progressed, Dr. Deneb's team has discovered another civilization living in a parallel dimension to our own. Two members of his scientific team inadvertently establish contact with the entities and learn that they are responsible for

Twelve Blocks

building not only one site but several sites around

the globe which hold different secrets to the

creation of mankind. Man's history will need re-

writing and a new birth of time for mankind is

about to begin which would include a positive

discovery of other intelligent life forms that share

our universe on multi-dimensional levels. The

advanced entities will catapult our mental ability to

100 percent capacity, enabling us to reach out

beyond our universe and into neighboring

universes with just a simple thought. The residence

of "**God**" has been located...

Jonathan K. Miller

Chapter One

The President's Plan

The discovery was made in the Arizona desert, on April

2, 2021, by two high school seniors who accidently

kicked a 3-inch antenna sticking out of the ground,

while searching for a ring that was tossed out of a car

window by a "now"ex-girlfriend.

The Oval Office, Washington, DC, 09:00 hours

"General Braxton, get yourself in here", echoed

President Sinclair from his office. As the General

walked into President Sinclair's office he responded

happily. "Good morning, Mr. President".

Twelve Blocks

"How are you and how was your flight General" the

President says as he pours his third cup of coffee. He's

been up since 2:00 am with a migraine headache.

Whether from excitement or worry was yet to be

decided. Big things were happening and he was at the

forefront of a major event about to unfold across the

country, and even the world.

"I'm good sir. The flight was long, yet relaxing".

"Well, welcome back to Washington! You look good
General!"

"Thank you, Mr. President, I appreciate that
comment, especially as I get older."

"Pour yourself some coffee and come join us. Is this
your first visit to the oval office?"

"Yes, Sir, it is."

"Well, I'll tell you, the coffee is better in this office than anywhere else in the White House. Tell me General, are you still lugging that dog of yours around everywhere you travel?"

"No Sir. Butchy went to dog heaven about eight months ago."

"Oh, I'm sorry to hear that. I know you were very fond of that dog."

"Yes Sir. He tolerated me when no one else would." General Braxton missed his dog more than he was willing to admit. After all, how could a General in the Armed Forces explain how he cried like a baby when his beloved pet passed away. As ugly as Butchy was with brown and white patches and short squat legs. Oh, how

Twelve Blocks

he loved that dog more than anyone could imagine.

Butchy was with him thru two divorces and was a

frequent traveler with the General. Only the best for

Butchy!   He just didn't have the heart to get another

dog yet. Maybe when he retired, he would consider

that option.

   "Yes, indeed, our furry friends are like that. General,

I'm sure you know everyone here." The General began

to circle the room to shake hands and acknowledge

each of the cabinet members and military colleagues

before finding a seat closest to the President. Some he

knew well, others were simply acquaintances.

   "Well, let's get started since we have a lot of ground

to cover" the President stated. Item one, ladies and

gentlemen. "As most of you are aware, the Arizona

project is under way. It was a stroke of luck that this

Jonathan K. Miller

magnificent, historical event happened on our soil. We are currently assembling an elite team of expert scientists, headed by Dr. Frank Denab, to investigate. Unlike the, so called, area 51 disaster, we will not be covering up the discovery of what we find out there and create another bone of contention between the government and the citizens of this great nation. I am hoping with all of your help, we can find out more about the planet's history. I have very high hopes of making a great deal of money from this discovery. However, something has come up requiring additional attention. General Braxton, our satellites have picked up images or rather traces of another archaeological find in Ethiopia. This is your territory!

General Braxton tensed up somewhat at hearing the words "this is your territory".   While serving the majority of his life in the marines, and as tough as they

come, this phrase placed sometimes more responsibility

on his shoulders than he desired at this stage of his life.

He was close to 60 and wanted to kick back and let the

young puppies rise to the challenges of being a senior

officer.   In fact, he planned to retire in six months.

"Now, we haven't been able to verify if this is

accurate, which is why I am assigning this to you."

President Sinclair continued.   "We have been in touch

with the Ethiopian government and a representative

has been dispatched and should have arrived by now to

provide us with information that may answer some of

our questions. Further, the science team investigating

the scene in Arizona will also be the team going to

Africa, provided the story turns out to be legitimate.

The scientist I have selected to spearhead the

investigation is actually a good friend of mine and I'm going to throw him a few bones to bring him on board. You, General, will be responsible for transporting the American team to Ethiopia. Take good care of them for me, General."

"Yes Sir, Mr. President."

"Good! There may be a chance that we can still salvage a profit from all this if we can work with the Ethiopian government. If this becomes a worldwide phonomena, and we believe it will, we will pretty much have exclusive rights to this discovery generating more revenue for us and potentially the Ethiopian government. Carl, what can you tell me about..."

The Oval Office Lobby, Washington, DC 11:30.

"Jenny, something big is going on!" Ethel half

-whispered.

" What do you mean, Jenny?"

"Well, they have been in there for three and a half hours, no phone calls, no disturbances! And General Braxton was here at 9:00am sharp!"

"General Braxton?" questioned Ethel.

"Yes!"

"From Africa?"

"Yes!"

"Oh my! How did he look?" Ethel exclaimed!

"Oh, just a like a Greek God!" Both Jenny and Ethel began to chuckle quietly. Ethel was in awe of General Braxton. The old saying there is nothing like a 'man in uniform' was Ethel's motto. She adored everything

about the General from head to toe and beyond!

"Ethel, who is that gentleman sitting over there?"

"He's from the Smithsonian Institute."

"Oh. Well, if there is something big going on, he

could be sitting there for a long time," shrugged Jenny.

"No, I think he's the reason behind all of this." Just

as Ethel was about to share more information with

Jenny her desk phone started to ring. Ethel had been in

the political environment for going on 15 years and she

can recognize a big event when she sees one.

"We are ready for Dr. Blanney, Ethel."

"Yes, Mr. President. I'll send him right in Sir."

"Dr. Blanney, the President will see you now." She

signals to Jenny to stick around until she gets back.

"Please follow me Dr. Blanney." Once she delivered the

Dr. to the President's office and returned to her desk,

she sees that Jenny is still waiting and anxious to hear

what is on Ethel's mind.

"So what do you think is happening Ethel?"

"I don't know, but what I do know is that it happened

in Arizona."

"Why would General Braxton be here if it happened

in Arizona? If it happened in Africa, I could see his

involvement, but it didn't."

"Yes, he is stationed in Africa, that's what boggles me

so much, Jenny! Africa is a long way from Arizona.

"Maybe they are reassigning him." responds Jenny.

"No, no, no, no! There are a multitude of generals stepping all over themselves at the Pentagon, just 7 miles away, vying for such an assignment!"

"No, Jenny, this is something else, honey!" Ethel's desk phone rings once again.

"Will you get Frank on the line, please?"

"Yes, Mr. President, right away.

Jenny signals Ethel and whispers, "I have to leave Ethel". Ethel nods her head and quickly begins to dial the number. She rings the President as soon as Frank is on the line. "I have Dr. Deneb on line 2, Mr. President."

"Thank you Ethel".

"Frank?"

"Mr. President, how are you, Sir?"

Twelve Blocks

"I'm good, how are you?"

"Cold Sir. It's 9 degrees here in Ithaca!

"Cold enough for an Eskimo!"

"How is your back, Mr. President?"

"It's certainly in better shape than the budget! Wish you were here to help me balance it." Both shared laughter over this comment reminiscent of their college days together at the University of Chicago.

"Well, Mr. President, I'm sure the budget is much more difficult than getting through physics."

"Frank, I need you for a very important project that will shake the world as we know it."

"I'm here Sir. What can I do for you?"

Jonathan K. Miller

"I need you to lead a team of scientists on a very special assignment."

"Is this about the Arizona project, Mr. President?"

"I see you've been following the news.Yes, it is Frank."

"Is this your way of getting me into your debt *again*, Calvin" More laughter emanated from both men.

"No, I'm giving you the job because you are the best and most qualified person for it."

"Thank you, Mr. President! Thank you very much!"

"Frank, you have to keep in close contact with me, personally, on this one. I am receiving reports on the Arizona site that demanded my finding the one and only man that I can trust. Do you understand, Frank?"

"I understand perfectly."

"I'm giving you the liberty of choosing your own team. I'm funding this project directly from my personal budget so I don't have to deal with the bureaucratic red tape on Capitol Hill."

"I understand Mr. President."

"Very well. Get yourself to Arizona, Frank."

"Yes, sir, and thank you!"

"Oh, and Frank, Ethel will call you tonight with a set of instructions. If you have any questions, there will be a special number for you to reach me. A package should be arriving at your door any moment."

"I'll be looking for it."

"Excellent! Good luck Frank and keep in touch."

Jonathan K. Miller

"I will Mr. President." Just as they hung up, the doorbell rang and Frank headed for the door as excited as a kid when he sees a new video game at Christmas time or any other time for that matter.

San Jose, California, 5:00 pm two days later...

The phone is ringing in the office of Dr. Karen Peterson. Karen hates the interruption as she is in the middle of grading papers for one of her classes at San Jose State University. She can't recall ever teaching such brilliant students as this semester. Some true mathematical geniuses.

"Hello, this is Dr. Peterson."

"Hi Karen? This is Frank".

Twelve Blocks

"Hey, Frank, what a pleasant surprise, how are you doing?"

"I'm doing great, thanks for asking. Listen, I just arrived here in San Jose and I have something important I would like to speak with you about. Are you free for dinner tonight?

"TONIGHT, she replies. You're kidding, right? You're here in San Jose?! Why didn't you tell me you were coming?"

"I called yesterday, and reached your machine, but I didn't leave a message. Thought I would try again when I arrived. So are you free tonight?"

"I can be," smiling from ear to ear, "what time are you thinking about?"

Jonathan K. Miller

"How does six o'clock sound?" he replied.

"Let me see what I can do. Is there a number where I can reach you once I check my schedule?"

"Sure, I'm at the Hilton downtown, Room 1232. You have my cell number Karen?"

"I do now that you mention it. I don't know what I was thinking. I'll call you back in just a few minutes."

"Oh Karen, wait!"

"Yes?"

"Is it ok if I stop by to see Joey this afternoon?"

"That would be wonderful Frank! He would love to see you."

"Ok, awesome, would you call him to let him know I

will be dropping by around 3:30 this afternoon?"

"Sure, I will. It's so nice of you to ask to see Joey. He

loves you so much. He doesn't have

too many male figures in his life these days."

"He's a pretty cool kid! My little buddy! I was looking

at that picture you sent me of you and him when you

two were at the beach, in Santa Cruz, last month. You

know, I noticed his nose looks just like mine. Karen

raised her eyebrows at Frank's comment but said

nothing. Frank continued on,"By the way", I made

reservations for dinner at 17 West, if that's okay with

you?"

"17 West! Wow, Frank! It must be a special

occasion."

"It is. See you tonight, Karen." Franks hung up the

phone wondering what Karen was thinking about at

that moment. Maybe I should not have joked about

Joey's nose, he thought to himself with a smile. If he

could read her mind he would know that she was

thinking; Oh, my, 17 West! What dress do I wear? Do I

have time to get my hair done and my nails manicured.

The very finest restaurant in town! Dinner with Frank at

her favorite restaurant. How good does it get!

However, the true reality in his thoughts were: HE

KNOWS! When did he find out, How did he find out,

who has he been talking to, where did he get this

information, OH-MY-GOD, did my mother tell him? He's

coming to see his son at 3:30, Shit, what am I gonna do?

Her eyes were silver dollar shaped, and she is in quick

"panic" mode. No wonder why it's 17 WEST! She

Twelve Blocks

immediately calls her mother.

It's 5:50 pm and Karen is ready with ten minutes to spare. She hears the doorbell ring and heads to the door with butterflies in her stomach and shaking like a leaf. She is ready, yet nervous. She purchased some new perfume on the way home. She always loved Shalimar, it was one of her favorites, and she indulged in the moment. She paused at the door, closed her eyes, took a deep breath, and opened the door to see Frank standing on her porch looking especially handsome in his black suit, with his perfectly pressed creases in his trousers.

Frank was speechless. Karen looked beautiful and smelled terrific. She could have won any beauty contest from San Diego to San Francisco. Frank was holding a bouquet of red roses in his hand, smiling and shaking like a leaf. It was high school all over again, he was

thinking.

"Hello, Karen."

"Hello, Frank." He handed her the flowers, and as she

takes the bouquet she embraces him with a warm hug

and invites him in. He could feel her little frame also

shaking as he was and knew in his heart that she was

extremely nervous about this evenings events. If he only

knew! The man didn't have a clue what she was truly

nervous about.

"You look so beautiful", he says. "Your dress is

incredible."   They stand there for a few seconds smiling

at one another.

"I can't believe you are here in San Jose, she says

breaking the silence."

"Yes, I can't either. I received a phone call from Calvin and…"

Karen cuts him off saying, "You mean Calvin, Calvin J. Sinclair, the President of the United States?"

"Yep, the one and only. You know, he still doesn't seem like he's the President to me. He's just, Calvin, the jokester I grew up with."

"She shakes her head. "Well, he is the President and that's a big deal. Having the President as your best friend is not the norm!"

"I guess it could have its advantages, but it hasn't thus far. At least it hasn't until now."

"The President sent you here?" He looks in her eyes for a moment and says.

"Yes, that's one of the reasons why I'm here. Now,

my beautiful Karen, are you ready to go? If I don't eat

soon, I'm going to start gnawing on something".

"Sure, let me get my wrap." Down the stairs, running

as fast as he could, came Joey almost running into Karen

as she started up the stairs to grab her wrap. She

meant to bring it downstairs with her, but in all the

excitement she forgot.

"Mr. Frank," Joey said excitingly.

"Hey, Joey," Frank wrapped his arms around Joey

giving him a big hug.

"Listen, do you remember our little secret, the one

we spoke about earlier today."

"Yep," he says, smiling from ear to ear.

Twelve Blocks

"Well," says Frank, "we have to keep that to ourselves, okay? The secret is between you and me, right?"

"Okay, Mr. Frank."

"You didn't show your mom the gift, did you?"

"NOPE!"

"Outstanding! Alright then, we'll talk guy stuff later!"

"Yeah!" he responded just as his mom was coming down the stairs with the biggest smile he had ever seen on her face.

"What are you two whispering about."

"Just some guy stuff, mom! You wouldn't be interested."

"Oh I wouldn't, huh? She realizes that that kid is just like his father! Thinking to herself, boy is this going to be an interesting dinner.

"Nope! Have a good time Mom" as he turns runs upstairs and says "You too, Mr. Frank."

"Okay" she says, looking at Frank like she caught him stealing cookies out of the cookie jar.

"What's going on with you two?"

"Absolutely nothing, my dear!" Karen doesn't believe him for a minute, but she'll play along for now. I wonder if he's going to tell me during the first course or the second course of dinner. Maybe he'll wait until desert. I'm going to need a lot of wine for this.

"Let's go have some dinner Dr. Peterson." Karen

nods her head in agreement and smiles at the reference

to her title. She leaves for a moment to tell the

babysitter that they are leaving and they head out a few

minutes later.

Less than thirty minutes later they arrive at 17 West

and were greeted by the valet who opened the door for

Karen. Excitingly she pops out and speed walks over to

grab Frank's hand as they enter the restaurant.

"Frank, it's been three months since I've been here."

" Really. Why? This is San Jose's best!"

"Because this place is very special to me."

Then it hit Frank what she was getting at. He brought

her here three months ago. "You mean since we were

here?" *She smiles,* he has remembered. She looks at

him with deep emotion.

"Frank, I didn't think you would remember."

"Of course I remember, Karen. It was the day I came back to life. She understood what he was referring to. They both had lost their spouses exactly three years to the day they dated one another. It was Karen that had snapped him out of the state of depression and he did the same for her. They had both decided to go out and try to snap out of the pain they had endured at losing their respective spouses. The tender and heated moments they shared that evening was much more than they both expected from each other. Saying things to one another that would never, ever be forgotten. It was clear to the both of them that their friendship had just changed. The lines had been crossed into an intimate relationship for good. He had just given her a heartfelt compliment that rekindeled all of those precious memories. She was so touched, she couldn't even smile. Her heart was suddenly very warm.

When they reached the table, the wine was already there waiting. A refreshing California Pinot Noir that he had reserved earlier that day. Of course, it was the same table they had occupied three months earlier as well as the same wine. She was not surprised, for he was very much the gentleman. What she did notice was that the butterflys in her stomach were now full size eagles ready to soar!

They began the evening with appetizers of scallops and poached lobster, pear salad, the best braised duck breast they had ever tasted, and a luscious dessert Souffle' Grand Marnier with Fresh Berries. They toasted often, laughed and smiled throughout the evening.

Being engulfed with the conversations and laughter, Karen totally forgot about when he would deliver the news of knowing he had a son with her. Not realizing that it would be jaw-dropping news to him as well. Frank decided to discuss the reason for his trip later, much later.

Djibouti, Ethiopia in the Office of the President of the Federal Democratic Republic Office of the State

"Mr. President."

"Yes, Olyia."

"The Director of the Protection Authorities Office has arrived, sir."

"Please bring him in."

"Yes, sir."

Twelve Blocks

"The President will see you now, Mr. Saharan." Mr.

Saharan walks into the President's office.

"Ah, Nilo, it's good to see you again. Please sit down,

sit down. Let me pour you some tea. I trust that your

trip was without incident?"

"We didn't have any problems, Mr. President." He

handed Nilo a welcomed cup of hot tea.

"Thank you, Mr. President."

"You have come a long way, my friend. I hope you

have good news to tell me."

"Yes sir. I do have good news."

" I am much pleased to hear this. Very pleased,

indeed. So...Nilo, is it true?"

"It is true, Mr. President. It is there and it is

enormous! We are establishing a perimeter as we speak

sir."

"Is there anyone there to claim the land?"

"No one owns that part of the mountain, Mr.

President. We are building a fence with government

signs all around the perimeter, sir. It will take

approximately three days to complete."

"Only three days?" says the president. He was

surprised to hear the short amount of time it would

take to secure the area.

"Yes, Mr. President. That part of the mountain is

steep and difficult to get to. There is only one road

going into the sector from the east and it stops about

three miles shy of point zero. From there, my men will

have to proceed on foot. The cliffs are rugged and

dangerous for the average civilian. We will clear the

area and build a road to the point where the road

stops. Once complete, we can then proceed to get our

equipment in with off road vehicles. There is only one

area that has access to the entrance and we blocked it

off!. We have already posted twenty-five armed soldiers

on 24-hour guard. We expect no problems cleaning out

the area. Mr. President. It is also true that there are

remnants of a path, but no one knows how it got there.

My men have found strange metals that are

unidentifiable. The locals are actually afraid of that part

of the mountain. This does make it easier to set up our

communications equipment without being detected."

"So, it is true. What did you do with the metal?"

"Most of the objects are buried deep in the rock

making it impossible to move."

"Cover it, Nilo!"

"Cover it, Sir?"

"Yes, Nilo, cover it?"

"Yes, sir."

"You have done well, my friend! Has the media been notified?"

"No, Mr. President. Thus far, only a few select individuals know about the site."

" Ah, that's good, that's good! Listen very carefully, Nilo. Over at the University, there is a scientist visiting from France. He is conducting a seminar for two days. His name is Dr. Collins. Dr. Ethan Collins. I want him in my office as soon as possible. Tell him Tepala needs him. He will know what this name means. Do not discuss this with anyone. Do not disrupt his seminar!

Wait until you can get him alone. Bring him back to me,

Nilo. He will come willingly. I want this to stay as low

profile as possible. Do you understand?"

"Yes, Mr. President."

"Very good, very good, indeed." The president smiles

and shakes Nilo's hand. "So, how is your family, my

friend..."

CNN News, Emergency Broadcast, 5:43 pm

A plane carrying 257 passengers, crashed into Mount

Elbrus at 11:00 pm Russian time. It is reported that

there were no survivors. The wreckage is spread out

over two and a half miles. Rescue teams are on the

scene. Mt. Elbrus is located in the Caucasus range in

southern Russia, on the boarder of Asia and Europe. The

mountain is perpetually snow covered with icecaps and

22 glaciers, making it very difficult to find the wreckage,

let alone any survivors.

Russian Executive President's Office

Chief of Staff, Belousov Yury rushes into the

President's office " Mr. President, we have found a

compound underground at the plane's crash site. It is

nothing like we have ever seen, sir!"

"What are you talking about, Belousov?"

"Mr. President, the plane crashed into a building,

inside the mountain and left a gaping hole in the

structure, underneath the snow. It is very large, Mr.

President!"

"Contact the staff immediately Belousov. Have them

return to the office today to meet with me most urgently. See if General Evgeny is still in the building."

"Yes, sir."

The president picks up the phone, "Levitskaya, please get Mr. Oleg back on the line. Then contact Mr. Tsukanov Nikolay at the Embassy. I won't have time to talk to him on the phone, tell him to come to my office immediately."

17 West, San Jose, CA.

"Okay, Frank, whatever it is that you are priming me up for, you already have me at a disadvantage. So, with that being said, can we talk about it now before I fall asleep from too much food and wine?"

Frank's elbows were on the table and his hands

Jonathan K. Miller

appeared to be in prayer over his mouth. He raised his eyes from the table to greet hers. "Ok, he says, but remember, you are still a beautiful woman sitting across the table from me. I am focused on finishing the night out, as I planned, so don't think business is the only reason for my visit."

Karen's heart seemed to stop beating for a moment but she managed to say "okay" with a half-smile on her face as she turned and tilted her head to the side. Waiting for his next words, she blinked and dropped her eyes to the table in anticipation.

"The President has given me the Arizona project." She lifted her head, her big gorgeous eyes opened wide. She was now staring right into his brain, waiting for more.

Twelve Blocks

"Karen, he said, I need your expertise with me on this one."

She screeched, "YES!" Her arms flew up in the air. All of the restaurant patrons turned to see what caused the excitement. Upon seeing her and Frank, they assumed that he purposed. Everyone was smiling and thinking that yet another groom to be had proposed to the woman of his dreams at 17 West.

Karen looked around, collected herself, cleared her throat, holding back the silliest grin of all times and calmly said, "Frank, I would consider it a privilege to be part of this project."

Frank smiled and said, "Well now hold on, let me finish. Joey is only 9! You may be away from home for weeks and to top it off, I'm expecting my team to be in

Arizona in two days. Can you swing that, Karen? It's a

very tall order."

"Frank," she says, "I don't have to tell you about the

importance of this remarkable discovery. Nothing can

possibly top this archaeological finding in the history of

mankind. Scientist are without a doubt lined up and

down the street and around the corner just hoping for a

piece of this. To top it off, you chose 17 West to ask

me!"

"Are you kidding?" Frank began to smile. He was

elated to see that she understood the significance of

the project. He had no doubt she would. She was the

best in her field. Not to mention, her success was

accomplished without even leaving the country. That in

itself was sheer genius! He would not have to vouch for

his decision to have her on his team of experts. The

science community has a high respect for her work. She

has been published fourteen times and is considered

one of the best professors in the State of Arizona. So, he

says, "are you in?"

She smiles, nods her head and says, "what time am I

expected to be in Arizona?"

He says,"10:00 am, at Arizona University. Your ticket

is already at the airport."

She smiles, "why am I not surprised."

"Okay, Dr. Peterson, it is time to change the subject

now that the business of securing my team has been

accomplished." They raised their glasses to toast the

night and took a sip. "I do have a question Karen. My

recollection is that you had a fairly big project in

Colorado a year ago. Word has it that there was an

accident with two of your team members?"

"Yes, it was unexpected, and should have been avoidable."

"How long were you there?"

"Seven weeks in all! The project was supposed to last three weeks. My mother was kind enough to bring Joey out so I could spend my free time with him.

"How did it happen?" No wait! On second thought, let's not get into a sad conversation. I will ask you about it some other time. On a happy note, Joey mentioned that you are planning on taking vacation soon".

"Yes, I was!"

"And here I am asking you to join our team."

"Frank, this is the team of all teams! I would cancel

any vacation for this! I'll explain to Joey how important

this is to mommy. Once he hears that I will be working

for you, he'll be asking for daily reports." Karen and

Frank both laughed at this thought. Joey could be quite

persistent when he wanted to know something.

Frank took another sip of wine and said, "Now, I have

asked you enough questions. I believe I am ready for

your questions."

Karen is in a playful mood and says, "how do you

know I have questions, Dr. Deneb? You think you know

me pretty well, huh?"

He smiles and says with authority, "I know more

about you than you think." Her eyes open widely for the

fifth time tonight. "Now what is that supposed to

mean?"

"Frank smiles smugly and says, "because I have also secured"...saved by the bell, his office cell phone rings. "Frank here!"

The voice says, "Frank!"

"Mr. President, good evening, sir..."

Though they had a wonderful dinner, Frank was unable to end the evening as he had planned with the most beautiful woman in the world. The President's call, "unfortunately", had interrupted his plans. Karen, however, had plans of her own but it would just have to wait until their work assignment with the discovery of the century, was complete. She had to prove to herself and to Frank that he made a good decision choosing her and that she was indeed, qualified to be on this elite team of scientists.

Chapter Two

Meeting The Press

Tucson, Arizona. 8:30 am

Frank is sitting at a red light, on a street corner,
heading for Arizona University and begins to reflect on
how far he has come over the years. Always dedicated
to his studies, helping Calvin get through physics, it was
Calvin that had introduced him to Joyce who passed
away three years ago from cancer. Who would have
thought that two countrified teenagers would end up
with two of the most important jobs in the world. An
impressive portfolio, attaining two PhD's and an expert

Jonathan K. Miller

in Archaeology and Paleontology. Now a Professor. A

little self doubt caused him to ask himself.   Who am I?

Inwardly he strongly replied. I am Franklin Albert

Deneb, born September 27th, 1953, in Hayward,

California. Currently teaching at the Paleontological

Research Institute. Author of six books focusing on

Paleobotany in the study of fossil invertebrates, and

author of three books focusing on the study of all

human culture. A member of the Society for American

Archaeology. Awarded the Paleontologist of the Year

Award by the American Museum of Natural History on

February 22nd 2019. Nobel prize winner, and

humanitarian of the year on June 16th 2020. Now a

widower, with two grown children, current residence,

Ithaca, New York. He ended his thoughts by concluding

that he has found another place in his heart for a new

love who is actually a past love. If he can get through

this project, he will pursue this hypothesis.

President Sinclair had asked Frank and his team of

scientists to hold a press conference about the

archaeological discovery on August 11, 2021, at 3:30 pm

on the Arizona State University campus. Dr. Barry

Bennet, Botanist and Frank's science documentary

specialist, is late. In fact, Barry is always late! Frank will

have to start without Barry and there will be a price to

pay. Especially since he is giving Barry a career boost by

selecting him to document this project. He was the only

one on the team that was questionable and now he is

late...again!

Himmel Park 3:15 pm

Dr. Barry Bennet is sitting on a park bench in Himmel

Park waiting for his wife's college friend Cynthia. She asked to meet him there because she has big news that she knows he needs but does not want to divulge the news over the phone. Cynthia has a sister who works at the White House in Washington and her sister verified that Africa has discovered a facility similar to the one discovered in Arizona.

Barry is looking at his watch as Cynthia walks over to him carrying a huge manila folder. She hands the folder to him and says, "You owe me big for this one, Barry."

He takes a quick look and his eyebrows arch upwards! He kisses Cynthia's cheek, tells her she is a god and darts to his car which happens to be double-parked on a side street with a yellow ticket on it. He grabs the ticket, gets in the car and speeds off. His cell phone rings. "Barry," he says.

Twelve Blocks

"Barry, this is Carla! Where have you been? Everyone in my office has been trying desperately to reach you."

"I know, I left my cell phone in my car."

"Well, where is Dr. Deneb?"

"He's at the University, where I'm supposed to be, giving a press release. I'm in the car right now headed that way."

"You are?"

"Yes.

"I have dire news from Washington"

"I bet I know what it is." Barry looks over and sees Carla at the light on Cedar? "Is that you at the light on Cedar, Carla?"

"Yes, where are you?"

"I'm at the opposite corner! Carla, pull over! I can get the information and take it with me.

"Ok. Hey listen Barry, the dire message is, there is an airplane waiting for all of you. The President is sending you, Frank and Karen to Africa!"

"I figured that was coming."

"Barry, why are you always in crisis mode?

"I don't know, Carla!" He puts his head down and reflects on his hectic life for a moment. An instant later, he pulls over to the curb, stops the car, runs over to Carla and grabs the folder.

"You better check the contents carefully! This stuff is very important."

Twelve Blocks

"Thanks Carla. You're the best." Barry turns around

and heads for his car. He hears his cell phone ringing

and answers the call as he gets into his car, "Barry,

here!"

"Where are you Barry?" Karen shouts."

"Karen, is that you?"

"Yes, Barry it's me! "Where the heck are you?"

"I'm on my way"

"You better be! Frank is having a cow!"

"I'll be there in just a few minutes." He hangs up

knowing that he has stepped into it again. He

remembers hearing about a movie with an absent-

minded professor and wonders if he is the same in the

form of a scientist.

Jonathan K. Miller

Karen shakes her head after speaking to Barry

knowing that he is trying so hard to do a good job for

Frank. He just needs to get it together or no one is

going to take him seriously. Barry has a big heart and is

the first to laugh when you crack a joke, but he needs to

change his ways in the future. Humor can only get you

so far and operating in a crisis mode most of the time

gets you nowhere. She makes a mental note to have a

conversation with Barry in the future about this very

subject.

Barry comes to a stoplight and takes the few seconds

to look at the contents in the folder again. "OH MY

GOD, he says!" The light turns green and he floors the

gas pedal. Barry finally drives onto the campus and

turns toward the Science building where the press

conference is scheduled. He arrives a minute later and

Twelve Blocks

finds a parking slot along the curb reserved for faculty

and he pulls into the empty space. He'll chance getting

a ticket. Beats Frank giving him dirty looks! He nearly

falls as he steps out of the vehicle and rushes to the

door. He peers inside the building to see if the press

conference has started yet. Damn, Frank is at the

podium at the far end of the floor and appears to be

speaking as all heads are turned his way. Regardless,

Barry decides to take another minute to view the rest of

the contents in the folder. He is shocked at what he

finds and decides that he needs to interrupt the

conference or bigger prices will have to be paid other

than his ass getting kicked to the moon by Frank for

being late...again! But first he has to call a number he

found inside the folder. The message clearly states that

the reader should immediately call the number upon

Jonathan K. Miller
reading the contents of the folder.

Barry makes the decision to make that call before entering the conference. The phone rings on the other end and a voice says, "Sgt. Banks." Barry pauses for a moment and Sargent Banks says;

"Hello, this is Sgt. Banks."

"Yes, this is Dr. Bennet, calling from Arizona University. I am here with Dr. Deneb. We received the folder with the information with instructions to call this number?

"Yes, Dr. Bennet. Thank you for calling, your plane is waiting and will depart in exactly 55 minutes. A limousine will be waiting for the team at the conclusion of the press conference. Your personal belongings have been secured and transferred from your hotel to the airport.

"OH! Ok, I'll let the team know."

"Thank you Dr. Bennett."

Barry glances through the glass doors and can see that Frank is introducing the team and he knows he is very, very late, but decides to take yet another look at the contents in the folder. Reporters are now raising their hands to ask the panel of doctors questions about the discovery, but he can't stop himself. He opens the folder and views something that compels him to open the door and open it right now!

3:30 pm

The man knows this circus was going to start at 3:30. He knows how I hate doing this stuff by myself. I am

Jonathan K. Miller

paying him way too much money to simply waltz in here

when he gets good and ready! I need someone I can

depend on, and not a scientist who is constantly late

and in constant chaos. Geez...I'm talking to myself

again.

   "Frank?"

   "Yes, Karen.

   "It's time to begin."

   "Very well...alright...I better get this thing going. By

the way, Karen, thank you again for joining the team. I

know you were ready for a long vacation, but I'll make it

up to you when this is over. I promise."

   "Well at least, you asked me to join the top

archaeological team and the biggest discovery in human

history. And may I add that you asked me in style. I would have been a complete fool not to accept.

"May I ask if everything turned out okay in Colorado? I know this is a fine time to ask, but we really never got the chance to sit down and talk about what happened. And I didn't want to make you feel pressured to tell me until you were ready."

"It turned out as well as could be expected. I'll leave it at that for now. Tell you what though. After this press release, you can buy me dinner and I'll tell you the whole story. Deal?"

"You have yourself a deal."

"Oh, and Mr. Barry Bennet will be here any moment. As difficult as it might be, don't be so hard on him. He's trying to please you as best he can, and I know he appreciates this opportunity." She smiled and winked at

Frank, and he smiled in return.

Frank has always despised giving press conferences

but in this case he has no chose. Especially when the

President of the United States, who happens to be one

of your closest friends, asks you to handle this as a

personal favor for him. He owes me big time for this

one.

He nervously steps to the podium, places both hands

on the top of the stand, and takes a deep breath while

thinking that this discovery will go down in history and

he will be at the forefront of this adventure. He glances

at the lobby door and thinks he sees (Mr. always late)

Barry through the glass and says...

"Hello ladies and gentlemen, and good afternoon. I

Twelve Blocks

am, Dr. Frank Deneb. I know that each of you will

probably have a lot of questions for the team and we

are going to try to answer as many of them as possible.

Please understand that what you are about to hear are

all recent developments and we may not have all the

answers. I ask that you please be patient."

"We are going to start out with a statement about

what we found. Please wait until I am finished with the

prepared statement before you start asking questions.

We may be able to answer some of your questions

within the statement. We don't have a lot of time, so let

us please begin. Can we all sit down. This room is very

small and the people in the back can't see unless you

are seated." Pausing a moment to give the audience

time to find their seats, reconizing several members of

the media, he thanked everyone and began introduce

the team.

"I would like to start by introducing to you the extraordinary science team who have been selected and assigned to this project. On my far left is History and English Literature Professor, Karen Peterson, from San Jose State University. Next to Dr. Peterson is Physicist and Mathematician, Professor Kyle Stevens, from Kansas State University. On my right is Archaeologist, Dr. Carl Harmon, from the Smithsonian Institute, in Washington DC, and Astronomer, Dr. William Cedar, from SETI, *(Search for Extraterrestrial Intelligence)*, and Botanist, and Dr. Barry Bennet, from the University of Alabama, who has yet to arrive. As you can see, we have the best minds in the world working on this project. These scientists before you are the chosen leaders of other science teams around the world, and will be directly involved with this incredible

archeological discovery."

"Ok"...pausing to gather his thoughts, Frank decides

to just dive into the flood of information written in front

of him. In the corner of his right eye, he can see

reporters already raising their hands like excited school

kids wanting to get their questions in first. As the low

tone of the whispering crowd increasingly rises, he

bellows out...

"We found what we think is a very old science

laboratory, approximately 4 ½ miles underground, in

the middle of the Arizona desert." Dead silence filled

the room. All arms dropped like pixey sticks. Suddenly

you could hear the air coming through the air

conditioning vents. People in the back, going to and fro

to the restrooms, froze in their tracks. They all looked

Jonathan K. Miller

like deer caught in the headlights of a car. Everyone

had silver dollars eyes, waiting for more words from the

Dr. In just that two seconds after spilling the beans,

Frank thought about an old twilight zone episode of a

pocket watch that had the ability to freeze time. What

he had just said stopped everything and everyone. If

only he could just walk out right now, while everyone

stopped breathing and continue working with his team.

But that was not going to happen.   He not only had to

continue, he had to continue without BARRY, which he

also thought about in that quiet instant of dead time!

Frank continued on...

   "We think it was left behind or abandoned by a race

of beings not indigenous to this planet, and to date, we

have no idea where they came from. There is also

reason to believe that the laboratory was an expedition

of some sort. We'll get into that later."

Pam Sheer, a reporter with CBN, a serious pain in the neck, who no one likes, stood up like someone stuck her in the butt with a needle.

"Dr. Deneb, Dr. Deneb?"

Anticipating her inability to stay in her chair for more than two and a half seconds, Frank cut her off before she began popping her chops. "Hold on Pam, hold on, let me finish! I said we'll get to all of your questions after this statement. There's much more that I have to say! Please indulge me, and be patient until I am finished." Now, it was Frank who had the silver dollar eyes, literally staring her back into her chair like a hypnotist. He had made a decision not to let the press take over this meeting two days ago! Especially, Pam!

She was about to speak again, but Frank didn't blink, he didn't continue, he stared at Ms. CBN for what seemed like hours. To everyone's surprise including Frank, she sat the hell down.

"The laboratory is roughly the size of a small city with a highly sophisticated transportation system, an energy producing system that we are not remotely accustomed to, and living quarters and food sources unlike anything we can presently comprehend. Now, before you ask, *NO*, the lab is totally non- operative. However, we have come to the conclusion that it was systematically shut down and can, I repeat, can be reactivated. We do have a theory on how to reactivate the labs power system. We are not sure what kind of power source it is. So at this time we will not attempt to activate its power source until we understand more about the technology. Though this lab was constructed

millions of years ago, the technology is also millions of

years ahead of us!   How do we know it's a laboratory?

To be as descriptive as possible, we have found animal

remains, plants, sea creatures, rocks, sand, and volcano

samples, all of which are perfectly preserved."

"We think the purpose of the laboratory was the

study of earth's chemical make-up. It appears to be

some kind of biological breakdown of our planet at the

atomic or even higher level. We found charts and

architectural blueprints of an earth species that has

long been extinct."

"There are things we know and even more things we

don't know about this facility. So with that being said,

we are going to limit the information we share, due to

that fact that we are still investigating the resources.

Jonathan K. Miller
We ask again. Please, please, be patient."

"Further, we are not going to use the same protocols that we have used in the past with this particular investigation. We think the public has a right to know about this discovery. Is this a classified investigation you might ask?"

"We are not classifying this discovery as a top secret, government or a military exercise, but because we don't know so many things of what we actually have down there, the government must put precautionary measures into play. Remember, this was only discovered a few weeks ago and we are going to do the best we can to keep you updated on the progress."

"Please keep in mind ladies and gentlemen that we have about 2 hours to answer your questions." It was time for the part Frank hated the most. We will take

your questions now. Ok, Pam, I see you're still busting

out at the seams, so we'll start with you."

Pam Sheer, CBN news, shoots her hand up in the air

as soon as Frank said her name and spits out her

question before Frank ended his sentence. "How did

they manage to build a laboratory so deeply in the

middle of the desert?" And this is why, Frank thinks to

himself, this woman is such a pain in the butt. How in

the H-E-L-L would we know. We weren't there! Geez-

oh-Pete! She seems to think that she is immune to

sounding stupid in public. Ok, a calm answer for the

sake of future funding.

"Pam, as far as the construction of the alien facility,

we don't know how they managed to do it. Why did

they choose the middle of the desert? For one, when

Jonathan K. Miller

they built this facility, we know the Arizona desert was

not a desert at the time of construction. However, we

think, at one time, it was even deeper than it is today!

Why this particular location is unknown. It may have

had something to do with what was lurking on the

surface of the planet at the time, or they were having

trouble with earth's atmosphere, Fact is, we just don't

know."

"Also, the laboratory is built with a material that is

unknown to us. We don't know if they produced this

material from our planet or their planet? The rock, soft

soil, moisture, pressure, heat! Nothing has affected or

penetrated the outer skin of the facility. The lab seems

to be wrapped in a cocoon-like substance, and it's

massive. The surroundings that protect this lab are still

protecting the lab today. We have not had a chance to

test the metals and many other factors yet. We are just

getting started on a very long process. But Pam, you

should see the scientist buzzing around like school kids"

Amazing stuff to watch!" (He moves on to the next

reporter),

"You have a question Greg?

"Yes sir. Is there any evidence of additional

underground structures?

"No, Greg. No evidence. We do, however "believe"

that there are more laboratories. I'm not at liberty to

discuss why we have come to this conclusion." With

that statement, the reporters began to rapidly asking

additional questions talking over one another and

making it impossible to hear clearly.

"Now, let's wait a minute before everyone gets too

excited about this possibility. The labs are giving us

information that leads us in the direction that suggest, I

repeat, suggest, that there might be more laboratories

on the planet. When we know more, you will. We are

currently looking around our earth now that we know

what to look for. We are just getting started people, I

can't stress that enough! I know that sounds evasive,

but, well, that's all I can say about this, so let's stay on

task about THIS laboratory! I'm sorry, I can't tell you any

more than that."

"Next question, please. Jen, you have a question?"

"Yes, Doctor, Deneb can we determine how long the

lab has been here? "

"Yes, we think it was constructed about two million

years ago, plus or minus a thousand years."

"How did you come to that conclusion?"

Frank hesitates for a moment thinking this is as good

of a time as any to get Karen involved. Looking to Karen

he says, "I would like to defur this question to Dr.

Peterson, our lead archeologist for this site?"

"Of course, Dr. Deneb. Our team has been testing the

minerals, soil and the rocks surrounding the lab. The

results from the test reveal the soil and rock to be dated

around the time Dr. Deneb indicated. Approximately 2

million years ago. To be totally accurate, we can't, but

we can estimate the surrounding soil within a few

thousand years."

"Dr. Deneb," says an unknown reporter, "you

mentioned that Dr. Peterson is the lead archaeologist

for this site. What do you mean for this site? Are you

saying you found other site?

"Yes, we have other sites." We have multiple sites, but they are not related to this archaeological discovery. We find artifacts everyday around the world! Nothing like this one but certainly worthy discoveries for us to investigate. We were very lucky that Dr. Peterson was available. To answer your question, this is the site that Dr. Peterson has been selected to investigate and that is all I am referring to as far as other sites are concerned." Karen is thinking how protective Frank has become since the enchanting dinner back in San Jose. She smiles inside without letting her emotions show on the outside.

"Travis, your question please."

"Yes Sir. Does this discovery serve a purpose?"

Frank is puzzled by the question and gives Travis a

peculiar look!

"A purpose? I don't understand your question. What

do you mean does it serve a purpose? Are you asking if

we understand the objectives of the species who built

the facility? That answer would be no, but we do

believe we have found a way to understand some of

their technology and a few of the projects that the

entities were working on. We have a long way to go. But

the overall objective of this lab is still quite a mystery.

Our scientists are trying to decipher their language and

number systems. Some of the data we found were

repeated on several tablets. We can only deal with the

facts as they are Travis. Now, from time to time, our

scientist may hit a wall causing us to have to

hypothesize with one another, to get us kick started

Jonathan K. Miller

again. But we can't document anything as solid

evidence until we have proof. Now, our educated guess

would be...well, we think the entities were interested in

making planet earth a home. Next question, please!

Grace?"

"Yes, um, with so many planets in the universe, why

do you think they selected this planet?"

"Well, Grace, we assume they wanted the earth's

resources. Another hypothesis Grace".

"We don't truly know why they came to earth. We

can only make assumptions at this point. As we

continue to observe other planets from our position in

the universe which is vast, water seems to be the key to

life. We are discovering more and more planets that we

believe contain water. What we don't know is what

other element may be mixed with the water on other planets. Water mixed with other elements and a technology far superior to ours, who knows what this combination can produce. It is all a hypothesis Grace. We're trying to piece this together as we learn more about their existence on this planet."

"Barbara, your question."

"Doctor, did you find any aliens?"

"I was waiting for that question to be asked. We didn't find any alien bodies or even pictures of any species inside the facility. The place was vacant. It was also very clean. No dust, particles, dirt, lint, nothing. They simply shut down and vanished. What we did find were packs of an organic supplement, that were freeze dried and liquids high in proteins. Of course, more tests will be conducted as our investigation continues.

However, what we have found gives us an indication

that their anatomy was similar to ours due to the

supplements we found. Further testing of the organic

material will tell us more. We will pass on this

information to you as we gather more data."

   "Pam, another question?"

   "Yes, Do you know how long ago the aliens were on

earth?"

   I'll be darn, thought Frank. A decent question from

Pam! He glances over at Dr. Peterson. "Dr. Peterson?"

Karen didn't like to give approximate answers, but he

still wanted her to give an answer because the question

was in her field of study. He knows that she would feel

uncomfortable having to answer a question that they

couldn't possibly know at this time, but this will be good

training for the future.   She looks down at the table,

crosses her fingers and says,

"We think, approximately 750 to 800 years."

Pam's eyes widened and she cocked her head back,

quickly saying..."What? And you don't think they were

on the surface?"

"We didn't say that, Pam. I'm sure they were! They

just didn't leave any evidence of being on the surface.

Not a single sign whatsoever. So we can't tell you or

anyone whether they have or haven't. With that being

said, we do think they were on the surface. Why did

they build a facility underground? We just don't

know...yet."

The front door to the suddenly opens, and Dr. Barry

Bennet appears. He begins to work his way through the crowd, stops halfway down and lifts up his finger, pointing toward the side of the stage as a signal that he needs to speak to Frank. Frank nods his head, and both Barry and Frank head for the side of the stage.

Pam seizes the moment to ask yet another question. "She yells out, what do you think caused the aliens to leave this planet and was there any sign or indication of why they left?" Frank is beginning to become annoyed with the CBN reporter, but decides not to let it get the best of him. He stops at the end of the stage where Barry is waiting and turns to answer Pam.

"There was a possibility that something went wrong. We believe that they left in a hurry. But, even in a hurry, they took the time to carefully shut everything down. They left the rooms intact, nothing on the floors, no open containers and nothing seemed out of place as far

as we could tell. We do think they left before they were

scheduled. We also believe they intended to return."

Pam jumps to attention. That *pin* is sticking her again.

"Why do you think that," she asks?

"Frank pauses about 5 seconds and looks at her, in

hopes that she sees his frustration and will stop yelling

out questions without being acknowledged. He then

says in a quieter voice.

"Because the…." Barry signals Frank that his

attention is needed immediately.

"Excuse me a moment"

As Frank approaches him, Barry begins to speak in a

hurried voice. The two scientists sitting nearest to the

end of the stage can hear what Barry is saying and their

eyebrows lifted as their mouths dropped and they

looked at one another in astonishment. Clearly the

audience can see that Barry has delivered some striking

information. Frank summons his fellow colleagues over

to the side of the stage and a conference between them

begins. The reporters become curious and begin to

make the usual false conclusions that the sky is falling.

As the scientists continue to converse, Frank walks over

to center stage and makes an announcement.

"Ladies and gentlemen, I've just been informed that

we have to cut this conference short. There will be

another press conference scheduled in a few days. We

do apologize for the inconvenience."

The audience starts to murmur and Pam says.

"What's going on Dr. Denab?" Certainly not surprised

it's Pam, he says,

"We have just received some information, but it has not been verified, so we can't give a statement until we find out more. The team has been summoned to investigate the information we just received. Again, we apologize and we thank you for your time."

Pam yells out, "Did someone get killed? Did you find some dead aliens?"

"NO, Pam," Frank replies. "No one was killed! And we didn't find any aliens, dead or alive. We plan to hold another press conference when we have more information to communicate. Again, thank you ladies and gentlemen.

The team hurries off the platform and disappears into another room in the building. Security rushes to the platform to stop the reporters from following Frank and

his team as they shout, "WHAT DID YOU FIND OUT?

WHAT IS HAPPENING? DID YOU FIND ALIENS? DID YOU

FIND A SHIP? WAS THERE AN EXPLOSION?"

"Alright, Barry, please share what you have learned?"

Frank questions.

Barry takes a deep breath and replies, "They found

another facility in Ethiopia! Smack dab in the middle of

Mt. Ras Dashen, 10,374 feet up." There was a moment

of silence as they all looked at one another.

"How high is Mt. Dashen's peak," Frank asks?"

Barry looks at him and raises his eyebrows, "14,928

feet,"

Frank looked surprised and stated, "that puts it at

4,554 feet deep. Which means 2 million years ago, it too, was underground."

Barry says, "yes, more than likely. But, Frank," he pauses a second, "these guys were geneticist!"

"Geneticist, how do we know that?"

Barry shakes his head and says, "just like we know who the desert aliens were. Samples, experiments, charts! They were splicing, Frank! Creating new animal species, plants, even insects!"

Frank, thinks for a moment and says, "Whoa, wait a minute, let's slow down, you can't possibly know that!"

Dr. Stevens, who has been quiet up to this point asks, " who is leading the team over there?"

Barry says, "Dr. Collins, and his team out of Paris,

France. You know what Collin's is saying about this,

Frank? He's thinking genetic alterations! I have pictures

of the lab. You won't believe it! They were creating

something!"

Kyle started shaking his head and says, "Collins can't

possibly understand the data from these beings this

soon, no way!

"He is a bright scientist, but..." Barry says, "wait until

you see the pictures before you make that statement,

Kyle, then give me your opinion. France is very close to

the African government. They gave Dr. Collins and his

team an unlimited budget to run this project."

"Dr. Harmon who has yet to chime in asks, "can we

see the pictures Barry?"

"Yes, once we get in the limo outside. There's a plane

Twelve Blocks

waiting for all of us at the airport, and Carl, it's one of

the Air Force's fastest jets!"

Frank's eyes open wide, and he says, "the Air Force

sent us a plane? And a limo?"

"Oh, yes," says Barry and escorts too!" Frank is

wondering how long it would have taken Barry to share

that they were taking a jet plane to another country.

Frank in shock says, "we have escorts? You're

kidding, right?"

Barry says, "No, I'm serious! And our personal

belongings were confiscated at the hotel and taken to

the airport. Can you believe that?"

"Barry, when is this jet plane scheduled to take off?"

"In about 35 minutes Frank.

"What else don't I know Barry?"

"Well, General Braxton has taken over the operation." Frank closes eyes, shaking his head and says, "Great! The news gets better by the minute."

"Barry smiles and says, "Yeah, thats what he said when he found out that you were involved. Frank contemplated choking Barry at this point, but then he would be arrested and never see the inside of the facility in Africa. Pity, it's almost worth it.

"Frank, the specimens they found are perfectly preserved." continues Barry as if nothing unpleasant occurred. " Some of them are still in cryogenics! Frozen solid with a power source that isn't even registering as electricity. 2 million years old and still in cryogenics! They think the power source is similar to nuclear but leaves no signature."

That's impossible Barry," Carl exclaims.

"Thirty minutes ago I would have told you that 2 million year old cryogenics was impossible too."

"Okay Barry, you got me there." Replies Carl.

"Frank looks up at the ceiling and says, "Did you say there are plants still alive?"

"Barry says, "not only are they still alive, but some of these species don't even exist on the planet anymore! They are long extinct!"

Frank is absolutely astonished. "Wow," he says!

Karen crosses her arms in front of her and asks the question, "Who else has been summoned Barry?"

"I would assume anybody who is somebody in the scientific community, internationally. We'll find out when we reach the airport. There is something else. They found human DNA."

Carl's head snaps around, "What are you talking about? Who found DNA? Humans weren't around 2 million years ago."

"The DNA wasn't 2 million years old," responds Barry.

Carl again says, "What?"

Barry, shaking his head says, "It was estimated around a million years ago."

Carl growing impatient with Barry says, "Humans weren't around a million years ago, Barry! Ok, this is nuts! How in the world can that be?"

"Yeah, we're asking the same questions."

Carl looks over at Frank as he asks another question

of Barry, "was there any *alien* DNA found?"

"I don't know Carl."

Frank reaches for Barry's folder containing the

documents and pictures. "Let me look at those pictures

Barry. By the way, where did you get them?"

"It was Dr. Collins."

Frank's eyes narrows as we pulls out the contents

and glances at the pictures, "What in the world is this?"

"Uh-huh, see what I mean? " Barry replies.

"Frank turns his head to the side and says, "do you

Jonathan K. Miller

think, what I think?"

"Barry quickly says, "Yes! I do!"

Frank says, "Well, we have a new goal, folks!" He pauses for a moment, then blurts out, "Okay, enough said, let's go. We have a jet plane to catch to Ethiopia! Kyle, Stevens, Bill and Karl, you all stay here and continue the research. We will keep in contact with you and compare the data we gather in Ethiopia. To quote lyrics from the old song from the mid-60s, Franks mutters "don't know when I'll be back again, leaving on a jet plane, da da, da da da da." They all smile.

Chapter Three

Extended Search

As Karen, Barry and Frank arrive at the airport and walk towards the plane, General Braxton steps into the plane's hatch to greet the scientists.

Barry smiles, looks over at Frank, "Ah-there's your buddy, Frank." Karen begins to chuckle at his statement.

"I will guarantee you dollars to donuts he's going to reach for your hand first," says Barry. "The General probably thinks you need to be placed in a padded cell with some duck tape on your mouth. He's gonna reach for your hand as if you were his new best friend."

Frank says, "Yeah, word has it, he's bucking for his third star. This is no doubt the most important mission his miserable ass will ever see in his entire miserable career." Karen makes a deduction that there is no love lost between these two. She pinches her lips tightly together and says,

"Wow, Frank. That's a lot of love you're displaying for the General. What happened between the two of you?"

"Barry pauses for a moment and looks at Karen, "I'm not sure that I would want to open up that can of worms right now, Karen."

"That bad, huh?"

Barry closes his eyes, shakes his head and says, "Sister, it ain't good! Karen looks at both Frank and Barry and wonders just how Barry could know the specific details and she didn't. It must have been

something huge because Frank's body language was

conveying contempt for the General. However, Frank is

always the consummate professional, and she expects

no less in his dealings with the General. She will have to

ask Frank for the details later. The General is waiting!

The three scientists reached the General who is now

standing at the base of the aircraft steps. The General

proceeds to step down from the plane with a look on

his face that seems to express sincere happiness to see

each of them. Smiling from ear to ear, the General

reaches for Frank's hand and pulls him in for a hug. His

big hand swallows Frank's hand as he squeezes it,

cracking three knuckles. The man stands 6 feet 9 inches

tall and is solid muscle. Very good looking, slightly

graying at the temples. The 22 medals and ribbons of

achievements pinned to his chest catch all the sunlight,

twinkling on everyone's faces. He has a high shrill laugh

that penetrates directly to your spine when the sound

reaches your ears. Just like chalk on a chalk board from

classrooms from the past.

"Well hello, Dr. Deneb! It's good to see you again!

How are you?"

"General Braxton. The pleasure is mine. Let me

introduce my colleagues. This is Dr. Karen Peterson."

"Glad to meet you, Dr. Peterson" the General replies

as he stretches out his hand to shake her hand.

"Karen says, "It's a pleasure to meet you General

Braxton."

"Frank then introduces Barry, you already know Dr.

Barry Bennet."

"Yes, I do know Dr. Bennet. Long time Doc. Good to see you, good to see you!   Hope you've been well since I saw you the last time".

"I'm good, thanks for asking."

" How is Cynthia, Barry?"

Barry was surprised at the question, he estimated it to be at least 9 or 10 years since they worked together. "She's doing great General! She's all grown up now and quite the young lady."

"She's what, 10, 11 by now?"

"No, she's 15 going on 30!" That comment brought laughter from everyone, especially the General who had a couple of kids himself who put him through the paces when they were teenagers.

"Wow, where did the time go?" replied the General. "I asked my wife that when our granddaughter April asked me to teach her how to drive last week.   That was one of my biggest challenges."

He smiled at that thought for a moment and quickly shifted the conversation and said, "Well, Drs, shall we board the plane?"

Meanwhile Karen whispers to Frank, "He's quite charming."

Frank says, "Give it time, the Grinch will show its ugly face. It's going to be a long flight, Karen."

"Well, I think he's very nice."

"You think everyone's nice. You adopted a dog that

attacked you and sliced your leg wide open."

She snapped her head around with a smile in her voice and asked. "How did you know that, Frank? Where did you get that information!? Did Joey tell you that!?"

"I do have my sources Dr. Peterson." Frank replied in teasing tone of voice. "I can always find out things when necessary." She smiled and continued to walk, thinking to herself, he does like me after all, and I'm going to kill Joey when I get back home!

Canter Elementary School, Camden, California, 1:30 pm

"Attention everyone! May, I please have your attention! I would like for everyone to sit down! I said, sit down, NOW! This bus is not leaving the parking lot

Jonathan K. Miller

until everyone is seated and quiets down!"   Mr. Gary

Clark, 5th Grade School Teacher, at one of the best

elementary schools in the district, is tired and doesn't

have much patience when it comes to the students

yelling and screaming this morning. He had an

argument with his son last night, and Patricia his wife

wasn't supporting his decision to ground Eric for

sneaking out the window at midnight to meet his

friends at the street corner. Heaven knows what they

were up to. He remembers when he did the same thing

as a teen.

He and his best buddy Michael left by the front door

and took his mom's car for a joy ride. They went to visit

some friends who lived nearby and the car stalled. They

had to push it most of the way home. The car started

when they turned the corner in the final stretch of

reaching his house.

They almost made it to the house, but it stalled again

just as they were pulling into the parking space in front

of the house. They jumped out of the vehicle not even

thinking that it was parked at a slight angle next to the

curb and ran to the front door. When they unlocked

the door and entered the house into the darkness, they

heard a voice say, "Who's there," and the light switched

on. Standing with a ball bat in her hand was Gary's

mom, Elizabeth." When I look back at that moment, I

realize how lucky all of us were that night. Of course, I

was grounded for life! My mom called Michael's mom

and he, too, was grounded for life and the afterlife. We

sure did learn a valuable lesson!

"That's much better! The ride to the museum will be

close to two hours, and I expect some order, is that

clear? "Yes, Mr. Clark." the students said in unison!

"And once the bus begins moving, no one is allowed to

get out of their seat until the bus comes to a complete

stop and I have indicated that it is permissible to do so.

Is that clear?" Again, the class responded affirmatively.

"Thank you." Mr. Clark turned to Bob Warren, the

bus driver, and proclaims, "we may now begin our

journey, Mr. Warren."

Joey pulls out a new laptop from his backpack.

"Hey Joey, I'll sit by you. Where did you get that?"

"From a friend."

"A friend, that's some friend! You stole it, didn't

you?"

Twelve Blocks

"I didn't steal it Keith. I told you I have a friend."

"I wish I had a friend like that!"

"Well actually, I got it from my mom's new boyfriend Dr. Frank! At least he's hoping to be my mom's new boyfriend. He gave it to me in exchange for information about my mom."

"No way! What did he want to know?"

"Just stuff."

"I don't blame him, your mom's hot! Joey punched Keith in the arm and they began to search for *Guardians of the Galaxy* to save Peter Quill, Gamora, and Drax.

Arizona International Airport 6:30 pm

Jonathan K. Miller

Welcome aboard! Everyone take your seats please,"
says a young Sargeant. "Can I get anyone something to
drink?" They all said no. She then informed them that
they would be taking off in 10 minutes.

"Please fasten your seatbelts. There will be one stop
at Dobbins Air Force Base in Georgia, for refueling. We
will get off the plane to eat dinner, and subsequently
taking off again at 1950 hours. There is water in the
compartment in front of you. In case of an emergency, a
breathing device above your head will drop down." She
began to demonstrate how the device operated. Within
a few minutes, the instructions were done.

"Sargeant, will you get that box under the side
compartment?" The General ordered.

"Yes Sir." After she found the box and handed it to

the General, she vanished behind the curtain at the

back of the plane.

"First class service! Very impressive General."

"Thank you Dr. Peterson." The General proudly said,

"Nothing but the best from the United States Air

Force!"

Frank adds, "But General, you're not Air Force! You're

a marine!

That sounded like a dig to Karen, but she decided not

to comment. What is going on with these two?

The General ignored the comment and handed each

scientist a four inch booklet with instructions to study

the materials. The information came from Dr. Collins,

and his team, complete with analytical reports, pictures

of specimens, mathematical tablets, consoles in rooms

located five levels deep inside the facility in Ethiopia.

According to the reports, the team worked nonstop for

9 straight hours under the direction of Dr. Collins,

comparing the data from the Arizona and Ethiopian

facilities and found many similarities. There was no

doubt, the specimens were the same.

Twenty-two hours later, three very tired scientists

and one General, arrived at an Ethiopian military air

base. Even though there were times when U.S. –

Ethiopian relations were at odds, the United States and

the people of Ethiopia shared a strong history as friends

and partners. Both have worked together to improve

services, such as health services, education, food

security, and expansion of trade and development in

the region, as well as peacekeeping missions in Somalia,

Twelve Blocks
Sudan, and South Sudan.

Frank saw a car motorcade heading for the plane

extremely armed as they taxied into a closed, fortified

hanger. As the hanger door opened to admit the plane,

the military vehicles entered on both sides. There was a

military tank next to the entrance moving into position

to intercept anyone who attempted to make a suicide

approach to the plane. The plane cruised slowly

through the, now closing, hanger doors. Frank looked

over at Barry and Karen who were wide-eyed and

standing on the opposite side of the plane observing the

same sight. It gave them all a different perspective of

the magnitude of the project from a country who took

no chances with a breach of security. It became very

uncomfortable in just the few minutes after landing to

witness such fortification and precautions, complete

with heavy artillery.

The General never moved from his seat. His eyes were closed, but he wasn't asleep. He was totally relaxed. Frank thought that perhaps he was acting in this manner as a way of keeping us calm. The military presence that we witnessed was certainly disconcerting. It reminded Frank of a visit to the Nassau Zoo with his kids when they were little and his wife was still living. The family was on a cruise through the Eastern Carribean with stops at St. Thomas, St. Maarten, Grand Turk, and Antigua, with the last stop in Nassau before heading back to their departure point in Miami, Florida.

They signed up for an expedition to the local Zoo. The bus ride to the Zoo was uneventful, but what a surprise when they arrived at the Zoo. Guards were posted out front, each carrying assault weapons.

Twelve Blocks

This is not something you experience when visiting a

Zoo in America.   Even the kids expressed surprise at

this unexpected sight!   We managed to have a good

time, but it left a sour taste in our mouths.

   As the turbines begin to wind down, the airplane door

opened and in walked a military Major. He greeted the

General and informed him that "HIS" motorcade was

ready. We knew that we were absolutely powerless in

this military atmosphere. We were along for the ride,

not to be questioned until the General was ready to

turn us loose. With all that fire power, no one wanted

to speak anyway. Clearly, we were fish out of water,

and the General was soaking up the glorious moment

like a Greek God! He knew we were and felt out of our

element. His voice was louder than it needed to be, his

head tilted back like George C. Scott, playing General

Patton! The man totally changed into a pit bull. He stood up and bellowed...

"Alright, saddle up everyone! It's time to get to the hotel. Once we get there, we will chow down and then get some rest before we visit the site. Our motorcade is right outside. Dr. Bennet, you and Dr. Peterson will enter the second vehicle. Dr. Deneb, you and I will go in the 4th vehicle."

Karen says, "Can't I ride with you two? I don't want to miss anything." She winked at Barry and smiled.

"No Dr. This is a security protocol situation. It is for your own safety." The General was stern and direct. The major led the way and they separated like the Blue Angels, flying in formation.

"I don't know about anyone else, but I couldn't wait

Twelve Blocks
to get off that damn plane and away from

Armageddon." says Barry! A side door to the hanger

rolled up and the vehicles rolled out.

Frank says, "How far is the hotel, General?

The General looked at him with a half-smile on his

face and replied. "Not far Frank, not far.

They reached the hotel in exactly three and a half

minutes! Directly across the street from the (**Dog-Gone-**

Airport)!

Frank looks at the General and said, "You have got to

be kidding me, right across the friggin' street! The

General just smiled and said nothing. Why they needed

a whole motorcade to jump across the street was

beyond them all!

Jonathan K. Miller

Since the federal government was footing the bill,

they were able to bypass reservations. The General

passed out room keys, actually access cards, to each of

the doctors. Once Frank arrived at his room he walked

to the window to take in the view.   He could see the

tank and its enormous gun barrel.

Two armed guards were positioned in front of the

airport entrance and a chain link fence separated the

property form the street. Frank felt as if they were

staring right at him through the window, from across

the "friggin"street! It was the General's moment to

show off his power, and NOBODY, but nobody, was

going to deprive him of his glory.

Not more than two minutes after Frank entered his

hotel room there was a loud knocking on the door. He

checked the peep hole, opened the door, and both

Twelve Blocks

Barry and Karen come trampling through the door

frame laughing with tears in their eyes They could

barely stand, they were laughing so hard!

WHAT WAS THAT ABOUT, both said simultaneously?

"No, Dr.! This is a security protocol!" Karen mimicked

the General's voice.

Frank says, "That, my dear doctors, was a clear case

of "I'm in charge here and don't you "freakin" forget it!

That is what that was all about! Do you see what I'm

saying now, Karen? The man is WACKO! Did you see

how his whole demeanor changed when that door

opened up? This is payback for having to take orders

from me 5 years ago when we had that nuclear leak at

the Seattle Plant."

Barry still laughing says, "Well, he'll be sucking up

when we reach the site Frank. He will have to rely on us

to make him look good on our reports."

"Yes and no," Frank says. "He'll reach the site, make

his presence known and wallah," G-O-N-E, like the

wind!"

"Barry replies, "Yeah?" Are you sure about that?

He won't stay around to garner more "glory".

"Oh, yes indeed! But until we reach the site, he's

going to be Rambo, Rocky, all the damn Avengers

wrapped into a single entity."

"Frank, are we having dinner with the good General?"

Karen asks.

"Yep! We're supposed to meet him down in the lobby

in an hour. Wherever we go, he has to go with us! His

job is to make sure we get to our destination and that,

too, would include where we "chow down". Once we

get to our final destination, he will vanish like a fart in

the wind."

"Has he vanished on you when you worked with him

in the past Frank? You seem to be waiting for him to

abandon you. It's quite clear you don't like the man very

much. Quite frankly, I was going to eat in my room, but

I wouldn't miss you two eating together for all the tea in

China. You two act like a bad soap opera." Karen said to

Frank. She was hoping the evening would not lead to

any arguments between the two men. Frank was

inwardly simmering that General Braxton was placed in

charge of this particular military operation. He would

have preferred General McDonald. He wasn't power

hungry like Braxton and a lot easier to get along with,

not to mention, he was well-respected amongst his

colleagues and subordinates.

Barry says, "I'm going to take a shower."

Frank replies, "it's about time, your clothes are

smoking." Barry rolls his eyes and exits the door.

"So, Karen, we never got the chance "again" to have

that dinner!"

"No, you skipped out on me, "again"!

"Yeah, well, instead of dinner, I have taken you to

Africa! Don't you think that's better?"

"I never said I wanted to go to Africa, Dr. Deneb."

"I thought every woman wanted to be whisked away

to Africa on a safari in the deep jungle, with Lions and

Leopards and Tarzan screaming in the distance."

Twelve Blocks

"Frank, you not only have the wrong country, you have the wrong romantic storyline as well. It's Italy and Nice, the Riviera, Paris, France and the Eiffel tower. What could you possibly be thinking?"

"I was thinking the jungle. You know, the part about Tarzan swinging in from a tree and stealing his woman away. Taking her high up in the branches, beating his chest, and claiming his manhood." Even he had to smile at this bizarre statement. "Doesn't that sound cool?"

"You have got to be kidding! Frank, Frank, Frank, you poor soul. You just don't get out much, do you? Do you have any idea how many mosquitoes are in the jungle? Snakes and Malaria, Hyenas calling their buddies to eat you, wildebeest stampedes. I'm a scientist! I see facts, just like you do! I am not the girl that trips over my own feet or is being chased by a man-eating Lion! I'm the girl that will pass your ass up getting to the jeep. I will leave your ass behind if you're late! Ok, that's it. I'm taking over this relationship. If you want to get it done right, a woman has to do it herself."

"What do you mean?"

Karen looked at Frank with her mouth half open wondering what kind of childhood he had. She then shakes her head, rolls her eyes like Barry did, and heads for the door.

"I'm going to go take a shower, too, she says. See you in an hour, Don Juan."

She leaves the room smiling and falls just a little deeper. She realizes there is a bit of innocence   inside of Frank. A quality she strongly admires in a man, especially in her man. Hmm, her man! Sure has a nice ring to it.

They all met in the hallway right on schedule, and went down to the lobby to meet the good General. To everyone's surprise, he was not in uniform. He had already ordered an appetizer and was stuffing it down his mouth. Frank had never noticed that the good General had such a muscular head until now. The man was clearly a powerhouse and a force to be reckoned with as they say. The General's assistant, Chief Master Sargeant Gomez, was at the next table pretending to act like she wasn't interested in what was going to happen at our table even though she was within ear shot of our table. The General slid his chair back...

Good evening, Doctors. Please join me. I took the liberty of ordering some appetizers. The food is a little different here, so I thought I would save you the trouble of ordering something that wouldn't move on your

plate." He smiled hugely as they all sat down.

"Barry says, So, what is this, General?"

"Standard rations young man!" Some good old

fashioned chicken wings, some fruit, mozzarella, and

cheese sticks from the plane's galley."

Frank says, "They didn't disapprove of you bringing in

food?" The General stared a Frank for a moment and

replied.

"As I said, it's a little different in these parts, folks."

The general looked over at Karen and asks, "Dr.

Peterson, what is your involvement with this team, may

I ask? What is your background?"

"Of course General." She cleared her throat. "I teach

English Literature and Political Science at San Jose State

University. Dr. Deneb asked me to help decipher the

literature found at the Arizona facility."

"I see. How is that coming?"

"Slow, but we're making some progress."

"You mean to tell me you understand that jibber

jabber, looking stuff?" Karen is clearly surprised that

the General is privy to the information. He must have

received clearance from the President himself to have

been afforded this opportunity.

"Well, yes, and no", she says tilting her head

slightly." It's a slow process, but my team is starting to

piece things together. The dialog, though it's a

language, is mixed with mathematics. Dr. Stevens and

his team are working with us to try and correlate the

patterns"

"Dr. Stevens, who is this Dr. Steven's?"

"I'm sure you remember him General." Frank replies. "Professor Kyle Stevens, Physicist out of Kansas State. You met him once in Seattle Washington at the nuclear project I spearheaded. You thought he was a teenager trying to get into the door at the Seattle nuke plant. You made him wait for 3 hours in the lobby until I got there. A simple call would have cleared him is seconds." This was a clear dig at the General which he chose to ignore.

"Ah-yes! I do remember Dr. Stevens. The baby faced kid. Why isn't he here?"

"Karen says, "Baby faced, yes, and very young, but a mathematical genius! It is just amazing how some people are born with the innate ability to do things that

Twelve Blocks
it takes the general population a lifetime to learn.

Absolutely amazing! He'll be working with us via

teleconference, once we get set up. It's hard to pull him

away from his computers. Treats them like children."

"Ah-yes, very good, very good... Well... shall we order

dinner?"

The general lifted his finger and 4 servers scurry to

the table from out of nowhere. They all noticed at that

moment that they had been carefully watched from the

time they entered the restaurant, and rightly so. The

general was responsible for the protection of every

American Embassy on the African Continent. The

general had a lot of power here. It was no wonder why

he demonstrated a God like attitude.

"Out of nowhere, Barry blurts out, "Ok, when do we

go to the site?"

"0730 hours tomorrow, says the General. We will meet here in the restaurant. Our motorcade will be waiting for us at the front door." I ask that you make every effort to be on time or the motorcade will leave without you."

It took all the angels in heaven and a few devils below, for the three of them not to burst into tears of laughter. They all looked at each other and bit down on their lips. The general suspected he had said something that triggered such a weird look from the doctors, but he was at a loss as to what it was.

Each doctor cleared their throat as if they "simultaneously" swallowed wrong. And Then It Happened...

Twelve Blocks

Barry, in a high pitch voice says, "I wonder, is the

"facility" next door?" They all lost it! The General was

dead silent staring at Frank. Not such a good way to

end the evening with the good General.

Chapter Four

The Arrival

NORAD: Cheyenne Mountain, Colorado Springs, 0300 hours:

Sgt. T. Bridges hands a trajectory tracking form to Second Lieutenant. A. Franklin. "Sir, I think you should take a look at this." Lieutenant Franklin glances over the form and questions what he is seeing.

Are you sure this is accurate, sargent?"

"Yes sir." Not only did it slow down but as you can see, it changed course to 11003.2 and was joined by a second vehicle that also changed to the same trajectory! I double checked this myself, sir."

"I'll have to call this one in Sargent." Lt. Franklin

proceeded to contact his superior office, Major T.

Dobson.

"Sir, this is Second Lt. Franklin. We are tracking a

couple of unidentified crafts that are changing course,

going around our vehicles at a speed far beyond our

capabilities."

"At what speed, Lt.?"

"Sir, we estimate the speed to be just shy of light

speed."

"Just shy of light speed! Lt., fax the information

directly to my house asap."

"Yes Sir." Anticipating the order, the Lieutenant had

Jonathan K. Miller

the fax ready to send. He faxed the form over while still

on the phone with the Major.

"You've got to be kidding me," he says to the Lt.

"No Sir, this report is accurate, sir. It was checked

and double checked."

"Ok, I'll take it from here, Lt."

Monarch Hotel 0730 Hours

They were all in the restaurant as directed by

General Braxton at 7:30 am sharp the next morning.

The only person missing was the General! A new face

appeared a few minutes later and introduced himself as

Major Anthony Walker indicating that he would be

escorting the good doctors to the designated site.

"Frank glanced around the lobby and asked. "Where

is General Braxton?"

"The General was called out late last night Dr. Deneb. He wished you good luck on your project."

Frank looked at the others, rolling his eyes saying, "didn't I tell you he was going vanish like the wind first chance he got. I rest my case. That man never finishes a project!"

"What a shame." Karen stated. Trying to lighten the mood Karen continued, "I was looking so forward to the conversation along the way,"

"Very funny, Karen."

"So Major," Frank says, how is this going to work?" Does that make you our babysitter?"

"Yes, it does, as a matter of fact. Doctors, if we can

now proceed to the car, we can leave immediately for

the site." As they crossed the lobby to the exit and

walked out into the sunlight, the doctors looked at one

another with their eyes popping out. They immediately

noticed, *NO TANK! NO ARMED GUARDS! NO

MOTORCADE!* They had been demoted from the

general's care. It was then that Frank realized that the

motorcade was not for their protection, but rather for

the protection of General Braxton.

"Major, have there been any new developments at

the facility that we should know about?" questioned

Frank.

I don't know Sir. The African government has

jurisdiction from here on out. They're pretty tight lipped

when it comes to talking to the United States Military.

I'm just here to transport you to the facility as

scheduled and secure your safety and well-being."

Barry says, "Really!? Are you expecting any

resistance?

"No, Doctor. I'm just informing you of my objectives.

It will be a ride without incident, I assure you."

"Isn't there usually more military personnel involved

when a project of this magnitude occurs Major?'

"This isn't America, Dr. Deneb. However, when I

drop you off at the gate the African soldiers will escort

you to Dr. Collins."

"Well, we rather expected…." Frank stated, and

decided not to continue his sentence and simply said, "I

understand Major."

"Did I miss something here, Dr. Deneb?"

"No Major, everything is fine." Frank paused and decided to say what was on his mind.

"Well, we rather thought that General Braxton was in charge, and well...we thought he was going to be handling the security."

"The major laughed. "Believe me when I say the General is definitely in charge. The General was under strict orders from President Sinclair to get you to Africa safely and soundly. You are here alive and well. He completed his mission and moved on to the next."

"NO SHIT!" Barry exclaimed.

"I see it's good to have friends in powerful places." Karen commented.

To ease their minds, the Major says, "The world has a

vested interest in what's going on with this project.

Each of you and Dr. Collins and his team are America's part of the contribution. You are on loan to Africa to study these incredible findings. This is an international collaboration, so to speak. You are considered America's finest in your respective fields of study.

"Dr. Collins is actually French and represents France." Frank shares. "But I get the point Major. All of us are in this together."

Barry says, "Well that's certainly good to know. I see this is going to be one of those projects where you only get a piece of the puzzle at a time and when it's time you fit all the puzzle pieces together."

"Yes, it seems that way", Karen says, "how do you guys put it, on an "as need to know basis." Isn't that how military people converse, Major?"

"Ok, we all need raises" Frank muses! "So, Major, um, to reiterate, we don't get any protection from our military? I understand that this facility is in an isolated area?"

"Dr. Deneb, the president *asked* you to investigate this site. He didn't *order* you to investigate this site Dr., and yes, you do get protection! African military protection!" They all looked at each other questioning the validity and effectiveness of this protection.

"Let me point out that the President is funding your visit here. You can be assured your safety is a priority. This is not a doomsday weapon you are being asked to investigate. To my knowledge, it's classified as an archaeological finding." The major was trying to understand their concerns and attempting to assuage their doubts so they could focus on the project at hand. While there were many years where the African government and the United States did not see eye-to-eye, the relationship is now solidified and there is simply no threat to their personal safety.

"Doctors, I can assure you that you have nothing to worry about." Unless you have received some kind of threat or have some other valid explanation that would cause you to be uncomfortable in your surroundings, there is nothing to fear. Is there something I don't know that I need to know?"

"No," says Frank. "Major, I have been all over the world doing what I do, and some of those places were questionable, as far as personal safety was concerned. I have never been here in this section of Africa, but I have heard about poaching in this region. This place is

isolated! When the locals get wind of this, the village

king who thinks he's the big dog in these parts may feel

he's entitled to his share and send his version of

warriors. I'm a little concerned, yes, about the

protection. People don't see what we see at these

places, they see opportunity. They see a chance to sell

old stuff for a high price."

"Major, this is my first archaeological discovery

outside the United States and I do have some concerns

about my safety. I have a child at home whom I love

very much. I don't intend to leave him an orphan"

Karen says. "I am relying on you to ensure I make it

home in one piece to raise my Joey."

Barry chimes in, "How serious is the African

government taking this project?"

"They appear to be taking it very seriously Dr.

Bennet." These guys are pretty good at what they do."

"What guys, says Barry! What guys are good at what

they do?"

"The African government!" replies the Major.

"Believe you me, they fight more here, than we do!" He

laughs but the doctors just stare at one other with a

serious look of concern.

"Look, you are going to be super safe. They have a

team of soldiers dedicated to this cause. They are

specifically assigned to this site. Besides, it's in an area

that nobody wants to be in anyway. No water in the

area, basically desert, very little vegetation, lots of

unwanted rocks that are way too heavy for oxen to pull.

Not much to offer the locals. That's why it's so desolate!

Not even the village Chief wants to deal with the area."

" Maybe not," says Barry, "but he will still think it's his! His rocks, his dirt, his lizards, his snakes!"

Karen says, "Oh, that makes us feel better, Barry! That's exactly why we think we need protection!"

Barry says, "Yeah, I feel safer already!"

"How long are you assigned to us Major?" The major's eyes shift side to side while he considers how he should respond to Frank.

"I'm ordered to drop you off and return back to base."

"Oh, that's just great! You've got to be kidding!"

"I thought you guys were adventurers." Major Walker said half-joking. He was getting tired of the whining. Doesn't being a scientist have some risk

associated with it?

Barry says, "Oh you're thinking about my brother,

Indiana. What do you think this is, The Temple of

Doom? This isn't a movie, man!"

"Frank in an effort to return the conversation to

some normalcy asks, "Have you heard anything at all

about the security and safety of the facility Major?"

"No, I haven't Dr. Deneb! I'm sure we would have

heard something if there were any kind of hostile acts.

If there were hostilities, you would not have been the

team chosen to investigate the site. Of that, you can be

assured! You see, none of you are expendable like we

are."

"That's comforting!" Mumbled Karen

"Well, I'm sure we'll be just fine," says Frank.

"It will be. All of you are a top priority." replied the Major.

"Oh, here we go again, we're top priority, folks! Everybody is watching us!

"Dr. Bennet, the world is monitoring your site, your work, and every step you take," continued the Major.

"Good!" Barry and Karen said at once.

There was an hour of silence that followed as they drove across some very deserted terrain. Miles and miles of countryside passed by and they saw villagers walking with large sacks on their shoulders and baskets on their heads beside the road.

Karen suggested, "Well, there goes that theory out

the window!"

" What theory is that Karen," says Frank.

"The desolate, no one cares about this area, theory, huh, Major? Looks like the entire tribal village is walking the road today complete with baby backpacks and goats on leashes!" Barry bust out laughing. The major simply shakes his head. They finally reached the base of the mountain and started to climb. Karen's ears popped. She had been making funny faces for thirty five minutes now, trying to get her ears to pop.

Barry says, "your face is very entertaining Karen. I swear you look like Red Skelton with that last one. Do it again," he says! He got punched for that remark. Who remembers Red Skelton, except for her parents. Her grandparents made her watch his show every week when she would stay for the night. They would laugh at

his silly antics and talk about it for days on end. She

never quite got it, but she didn't like the Three Stooges

either.

"How do I look now," she says?

The major looked over at Frank and says, "Are they

brother and sister?"

Frank shakes his head no, shrugs his shoulders as if to

say he's given up on both of them. But he can't resist

making a comment and says….

"Barry is related to Jimmy Duranty. Same nose and

ears." The Major chuckled softly.

The site was only 5 minutes away. To kill time, Frank

wrote a note and handed it to Karen in the back seat. It

read, *Joey gave me a picture of a little girl in braces, can*

I keep it?

She yells out, **"WHAT?"** Barry jumped in his seat!

"Doctors, we have arrived at our destination" the Major suddenly announced. "Dr. Collins will greet you at the facility entrance. A jeep is in route and will take you the rest of the way."

"Wait! You're gonna just leave us here," says Barry?

The Major looked at Barry and said, "All of your equipment was airlifted to this site last night. You are all set. The jeep will pick you up in approximately three minutes. You will be fine!"

They all thanked the Major and hopped out of the vehicle. They were left at the perimeter gate. Karen

Jonathan K. Miller

turned with the intent of questioning Frank about his

note when he decided to strike up an official

conversation with Barry about some reports he needed.

She decided to let it go for now. She knew that he was

attempting to avoid being interrogated.

Finally a moment of silence and Barry says...

"Hey, if we are such a high priority, then how come

WE weren't airlifted up here. And how come we were

dropped off to fend for ourselves. It's like sheep being

led to a slaughter?"

"Good question," said Karen looking over at Frank

with darts in her eyes." Maybe you can ask your buddy

Calvin, in the White House! Looks to me like our

equipment has a higher priority level than we do!"

"Very funny, guys," says Frank as he smiles looking

down at their equipment.

Karen sees the opportunity and decides to jump on it,
but then spots a car in the distance,

"Look, somebody's coming," she says. They stand
there like school kids waiting for the bus. Frank leans
over to Karen and whispers, "Did you ever get that mole
taken off?" Then steps away like he was stung by a bee,
a BIG BEE!

That "mole", she thinks, what is he talking about?
Suddenly, Karen's eyes become as big as a full moon!
She snaps her head around, Franks takes a few more
steps toward the oncoming jeep.

"I *AM GOING TO KILL THAT BOY AS SOON AS I SEE
THE LITTLE SHIT!*" How did he find out? The little brat!
Then it hits her like a bright light! Joey found my

childhood diary!

"He must have found my diary," she says out loud not realizing it.

Barry turns around and looks at her. "What are you talking about," he says.

"Frank," she says sternly! Barry's eyes grow big when he sees the death rays coming from Karen's eyes!

An African Sargent, in an open jeep pulls up.

"This isn't over, Frank," she says! Frank looks at her and tilts his head just like Karen does when she is thinking and says,

"Karen, what on earth are you talking about?" She squints her eyes and tightens her lips and says,

"You will not survive this! Joey will not survive this. Now

Twelve Blocks

I know what you two were up to. I know what's going on, and so help me, both of your numbers have come up." She puts two fingers up to her eyes and points them at Frank. She smiles and shakes her head slowly. Frank is now completely in love! Barry is all confused....as usual!

   With a heavy accent the small man in the jeep greets the group of scientists and introduces himself as Sargent Tomba Pabuto. Very polite, short at 5 feet 2 inches, balding, and dressed in military fatigues. A .45 caliber was strapped to his side. The Sargent stopped the jeep so abruptly that a cloud of dust covered them in an instant. Sargent Pabuto didn't even react to the dust. He was already covered from head to toe (or boot). He stated he was taking them to the underground facility. He stood there and smiled at them

Jonathan K. Miller

for a moment, then grabbed the higher priority equipment and loaded it into the back of the jeep. He had a very strong underarm smell that was **un-be-liev-able**! Frank was thrilled to be in the front seat. Barry and Karen stared at each other mentally praying for a gas mask. It was a long 15 minutes of duckin' and dodgin' the downwind draft of that musky odor bombarding their noses. There was zero relief! The very second the jeep came to a halt, they both popped out of their seats like Pam, the CBN reporter.

"GEEZ-ALL-MIGHTY!" Karen proclaimed.

"Barry couldn't be outdone and yelled out, **SWEET JUDAS BOOTY!**

Frank stood there smiling, "Is there something wrong doctors?"

Twelve Blocks

"OH MY GOD!" was all that Karen and Barry could say. Frank was laughing so hard he could hardly see.

The Sargent seemed oblivious to their antics or he just didn't care. "This way," he said. None of them lagged behind as they were trying to avoid the same punishment they endured a moment ago.

It was impossible to hold a conversation in the jeep with dust swirling around, but now the Sargent was able to converse with the doctors.

"How was your trip to our country?" He was so very polite and soft spoken and Karen felt a little guilty about her comments and looked over at Barry to see if he showed any of the same remorse. Barry was focused on keeping pace with the group, and she's not sure if he even heard the conversation.

"Frank finally responded to the question. "The trip was long but we were mostly comfortable until we got into the jeep with the Major to get here. That was some rough terrain!"

The Sargent expressed his apologies. "I am sorry to say that our roads are not paved. We really need to do something, but the costs are exorbitant, and we have other priorities for now. Perhaps one day this project will be accomplished. Can I get you something to drink?"

Karen felt like a real heel, shaking her head, disappointed with herself.

Barry knew what she was thinking and lightly elbowed her in the side, smiling, and jokingly said, in a quiet voice, "You're evil and need to be destroyed!" She chuckled and put her head down looking at her dusty

shoes. All of a sudden her mind went back to Frank

asking her about the mole, which was on her butt. Joey

may be her son, but she intended to make the little

varmint pay for his loose lips.   And Frank, he was going

to pay big time. Then it dawned on her. **HEY, WAIT!!**

How in the hell did Joey know about that mole? That

wasn't in the diary! Barry noticed Karen scrunching her

face, pursing her lips again, and he tapped her hand and

whispered, "what's going on with you and Frank?"

She shook her head and said "nothing, nothing at all!"

He almost thought he heard her growl.   Whatever

Frank did, the gig was up!   He was dead meat!

They arrived at the facility a few minutes later. The

Sargent opened the corridor door and everyone

stepped into the room. It was massive. Not quite as big

Jonathan K. Miller

as the Carlsbad Caverns in New Mexico, but

nonetheless, huge. When the door closed behind them,

and the lights clicked on, there wasn't a single sound. It

was totally, and eerily silent just like the caverns. They

all picked up on the silence immediately. The room had

a hollow concave ceiling, it was well lit, with lights

embedded in the ceiling. The sergeant indicated that

the temperature was stabilized at 65 degrees

fahrenheit. The floor was smooth and began to angle

downward as they continued into the cave. They

walked 100 feet. The more steps they took, the steeper

the angle became until they reached a flight of steps.

The steps were soft, like thick 3 inch carpet, but it

wasn't carpet. The staircase was 60 feet wide. They

descended 30 feet before reaching the bottom of the

stairs. At the bottom of the stairs the floor began to

angle downward once again for another 20 feet, then

flattened out for 12 feet. They approached a door that

was approximately 15 feet tall. The Sargent opened the

door and there stood Dr. Ethan Collins smiling from ear

to ear with his arms stretched out to Frank. Ethan was

the team leader of this expedition and resided in Paris,

France. World renown and a good reliable friend! Both

Ethan and Frank taught at the University of Chicago in

their early years. They were pleased to once again be

reunited on a project together.

Ethan reached his hand out to Frank. "How are you

Frank?"

I'm good Ethan, and it's so good to see you. How

have you been since we last met?"

"Very tired, but hanging in there Frank."

Frank and Ethan said in unison, "It was there that we hung first!" Too which they both laughed and slapped each other on the back.

"What was that all about?" Karen asked.

"Barry being somewhat knowledgeable at times said, "You really don't want to know. It's one of the stupid things we used to do in college!"

Ethan says, "Thank you, Sargent. I've got it from here. Thank you for your assistance. It is indeed appreciated. Sgt. Pabuto nodded his head and exited back through the tall door. "What a nice, nice man," Karen said.

"That's not what you said about the man a few minutes ago!" Barry said.

Twelve Blocks

"Barry, one of these days, I'm going to hit you in the head with a giant rock!"

Ethan who is quite anxious to share his findings and leads everyone into his office.

Still needing to do introductions, Frank says, "Ethan, this is Dr. Karen Peterson. Karen teaches at San Jose State."

"Yes, I'm familiar with your work, Dr. Peterson Karen and I've read your Bio. Very impressive. Welcome aboard!

"Thank you Dr. Collins, and please, call me Karen."

" My pleasure, and please call me Ethan."

"Nice office, Ethan."

"Thanks Frank. Do you notice anything special about

the walls?" Karen and Barry walk over to the wall and

touch it." Karen steps back and looks oddly back at the

other doctors.

"Go on, touch it again." She reached up and touched

the wall for the second time. With her eyes open wide.

She says, "It's warm."

"Yes, it is." Barry, give a hard punch to the wall."

Barry says, "what?"

"Hall off and punch it as hard as you can." Repeats

Ethan. "Trust me, you won't hurt yourself".

"Barry says. "Alright." He makes a fist and strikes

the wall as hard as he can, trusting Ethan.

The wall immediately changes texture similar to a soft

silicon with the impact absorbed.

Twelve Blocks

"WHAT THE…" Barry exclaims.

"Yes," Ethan says! "Can you believe that?"

How in the world could that happen, Ethan?   Karen

asks.

"We have no clue yet. Touch it again, Barry. This time

touch it non-aggressively. The wall was solid as a rock

when Barry obliged Ethan."

Barry says…"this is amazing! This is absolutely

amazing."

"Yes, the walls react to movement. The walls are

aware of everything that makes contact. It's like it has

consciousness, like it's alive.

Frank says, "Have you taken a sample to test the

material Ethan?

"No! We can't remove even a small sample. It doesn't react to knives, saws, diamond blades, spikes, or fire. Nothing can penetrate it. Look closer, no edges, no corners, but yet it has a shape, almost like an igloo. It doesn't even have a smell. Now check this out. Frank, throw that cup of water on the counter at the wall."

Frank tosses the water. The wall literally absorbed every drop upon contact! No splash, no spills. The water was sucked right into the wall instantaneously!

Barry says, "WHAT the"

Talk about a house maid! That's astonishing! Karen is mesmerized and can't take her eyes off the wall.

"Frank says, Incredible! The facility in Arizona is not constructed out of this material."

"Frank. I think the structure in Arizona was built

thousands of years before this one. We believe they left

and came back with a new and improved technology.

The data you sent me reveals a similar style, maybe

even some of the same elements, but nonetheless,

improved. Let's look at your data and compare. Have

you all had a chance to go over the data I sent?"

   "Yes, we have." Frank answered for his team. "None

of it makes any sense, but, we reviewed everything."

   "I have to tell you what the buzz is with this

information in your hand. My opinion is that this is

going to change everything we know about who we

are." Ethan is clearly excited about this prospect and

the rest of the team is sharing his enthusiasm.

   "Or better yet," says Frank, "what we are."

   "It answers why we're so mentally different from

everything else that lives on earth as you will find out

later today," says Ethan.

Frank asks, "How many other species did you find like

us?"

"A total of 52. Some of the specimens had DNA

strands we have never seen before. Take a look at this

frame."

Frank said, "Karen, Barry, look at this!

Ethan handed them another picture to look at and

asked. "What do you make of this?"

Barry was the first to respond. This looks....reptilian

and....insect!"

" Correct Barry. Impossible, right?"

In astonishment, Karen asked, "What you just handed

us indicates some alien is created from 52 different

species?"

"According to the data, yes, that is exactly what it

indicates, but they didn't combine the DNA strands of

humans."

Barry said, "Who conducted the test."

"Brad Templeton's team out of France, using a

supercomputer from the NASA science institute. Frank,

wait until you see them."

"See who Ethan?" Frank replies.

"These are things that aren't from this planet, that's

for sure! None of them are from earth that we can tell.

The compositions are similar, and they share some of

the same DNA strands, but not from earth!"

Jonathan K. Miller

Karen asks, "Did we dust the labs for prints?"

Prints? No Karen, they must have had a purification protocol we can't even imagine. You witnessed how the wall swallowed up that cup of water. We didn't find a speck of dirt, not a single print, hair follicle, lint, or saliva. I don't think they even farted in the place! Nothing. Nada. Absolutely nothing at all!"

Frank says, "Word has it, Ethan, that you think these aliens seeded the earth?"

Ethan replies, "Yes, I do! At least I think so. Of course we don't know why? Or shall I say we don't have proof of why."

Barry says, "What in the h-e-double L does that mean?"

Twelve Blocks

"It means we had a breakthrough of comprehending some of their language! The data is actually starting to make some sense to the computers." Ethan says excitedly.

"Come again," pipes in Barry?

"Our linguist had a breakthrough. As we speak their journals are being deciphered. For the most part we believe they had telepathic capabilities, and they did document things. Maybe to send them back to where they came from originally. We don't understand a lot of the mathematics and engineering and the language patterns are quite different. But we do know that the lab you found in the Arizona desert appears to be built by the same aliens in Africa. We believe the geneticists in the African facility were the advanced team. The second unit, so to speak. They weren't just testing at this facility, they were ready to deliver and probably

did."

"Deliver! Deliver what?" said Frank?

"Us Frank, and other species we consider to be

earthlings! History did reveal that humans were first

discovered here in Africa."

Suddenly, Larry Stanton, an intern on Ethan's team,

and a military officer appeared at Ethan's door.   Good

afternoon, Dr. Collins."

"Good afternoon, Larry, what's up?"

"Just delivering the mail Dr. Collins." He dropped the

mail on the desk and departed in a matter of seconds.

Ethan stands up and said, "Everyone, I want to show

you something that you will find of interest. Please

follow me. We're going to step into the room across the

hall, and I want you to tell me what you feel."   They

crossed the floor and stepped into the room behind

Ethan.

Frank says, "Ethan, what is that low hum?"

"We don't know yet, Frank. The frequency tone is too

low. "We don't even know the direction it's coming

from. It seems to be emanating right through the walls!

As we moved through the hallways, the humming

became much louder until Ethan yelled, "HEY!" The

humming stopped at the sound of his voice. "It's like

crickets in the night when they hear something. The

humming stops, then picks up again when it's silent. I

want you to tell me as we move deeper through the

corridor what you make of it. As a matter of fact, tell me

exactly what and how you feel as we move deeper into

the facility."

Before we do that, Ethan, I need to ask you a question, Frank says. Would you mind stepping out into the hall for a minute?"

"Sure Frank."

Once they reach the hall, Frank asks Ethan. "Ethan, how did you get this job?" Ethan takes a minute to answer him, then says, "the Ethiopian president offered it to me. I was doing a seminar at the university in Paris and he sent a senior staff member to tell me what was going on. Of course, I jumped at the opportunity, who wouldn't. Why, Frank?

"My government seems to think there is more information about this whole thing. Like maybe the Ethiopian government is holding back information". Is that all, Ethan? Is that all you truly know?"

"What do you mean is that all, Frank," he says with a somewhat defensive tone in his voice. This is me you're talking to! "What more would there be?"

Frank recognized that Ethan was becoming defensive and backed off. "Oh it's nothing, Ethan. I'm sorry if I sound suspicious. I'm under a lot of pressure and there are several high powered people in Washington with a microscope on my back, depending on me. I just want to make sure you and I are on the same page with the direction of this project".

"Why wouldn't we be Frank? Of course we are on the same page."

"Ok, buddy, again, I'm sorry if I sounded a little suspicious. You have been a true friend and I appreciate you. Let's go finish detailing this place."

Ethan smiles and throws his arm around Frank and

they rejoin the others.

Chapter Five

Laboratory Enclosures

The party descended down a narrow pathway with just enough room to walk single file. The hall was only 4 ½ feet tall and arch shaped at the top. They reached a doorway, and upon opening the door, they entered into a room with a staircase going down to level 3.

As they descended, Ethan asked, "Do you notice anything thus far?"

Karen replied, "Yes, there are no doors, no locks, very few corners, and no color patterns."

Ethan says, "Ok, follow me" he said as reached the bottom of the staircase. They looked around and saw several doors, all of which were closed. "Let's start here on the right in what we think is a decontamination chamber." He opened the door and a humming sound could be heard.

Barry remarks upon hearing the humming, "Oh, man, what is that sound!"

"The hum is a little louder than before," Karen observes.

"Everyone, examine your hands." Says Ethan.

"What the heck is this? Asks Barry.

"Look at the bottom of your shoes?" Says Ethan. "The further you go into this room, and the next two rooms, the cleaner you become. The bottom of your shoes are in contact with the floor. The molecules in your shoes have been altered! Move forward, please."

"Well, I'll be darn! Would you look at this! How in the world is this happening?" Frank asks.

It's one of those moments where the hair is standing on arms, and everyone is alert, but curious about their surroundings. No one seems to notice at first that their clothing is totally transparent. The floor was soft like standing on a three-inch cushion, but totally supportive to movement. They all noticed it was easier to breath. They all felt 20 pounds lighter and moved quicker than normal speed.

"Believe you me, Frank," Ethan replies, "if I had that answer, I would be the richest man alive!"

Barry says, "I do feel my clothes, yet they are transparent. I know that is not a scientific statement but, I can't describe it in any other way, and it's getting

warmer in here. My skin is tingling, my face feels...wet."

Karen remarks with a bit of annoyance, "Ethan, you

could have given us a little warning about the clothing."

Ethan replied, "You're absolutely right Karen. I was

thinking that we are scientists first and foremost, and

not considering the human factor.   Please forgive me. I

do apologize. I wanted to see your initial reaction when

I brought you down here. Here, let me get some lab

coats from the closet specially coated with a metallic

fabric to prevent transparency. We stored some in this

room just for this reason. Each of you are welcome to

grab one. Although I don't anticipate any similar such

encounters, I'll make sure that I warn you in the future.

Now, once you step back into the hallway, you and your

attire will be completely decontaminated!" Karen

acknowledged his apology with a slight nod of the head.

They exited the room back into the hallway as Ethan requested and followed Ethan for another 10 feet.

"Karen says, "Does this mean you'll be able to see our bones in this next room?"

Ethan laughs and says, "No, but tell me how you physically feel. Your scientific explanation of how you feel that is."

They arrived at the next door and hear another mysterious sound coming from the room. This hum had a lower pitch, and it is much louder than the previous chamber. This chamber had a sliding door that opened automatically when they walked up to it. They entered the room to find a console on the far side of the room with several control switches on two separate tiers.

Jonathan K. Miller

There were 8 single stem, bar stools in front of the console. The chairs were molded into the floor without any nuts, bolts or screws visible. A 19-inch viewing inch screen, equivalent to a television screen was in the middle of the console. On the west wall was a 35-inch viewing screen and nothing else. On the south side of the room were seven, six foot cabinets. As they entered, they all felt slightly dizzy and a bit sick to the stomach. Their vision was somewhat blurred. The temperature was 29 degrees farenheight. All their clothing had turned completely white and was vibrating on their bodies as if the clothing had come to life.

Barry says: "Oh, my God!"

"Your vision will adjust Barry, "says Ethan, "but the nausea and dizziness may remain, depending on your body's ability to correct itself."

Twelve Blocks
"Can you turn down the humming?"

"No Frank, I can't." Ethan says as he shakes his head no. "We haven't found a way to do that yet. We don't know which switch to use as of yet. I can't take the chance and push a button that proves to be life threatening or cause some kind of calamity.

There is another chamber identical to this one down the hall. I have a team in there now." Ethan puts his hand on Frank's shoulder to get his undivided attention. "Frank, there is more. Let's move over here, and take a look at this." Ethan moves closer to the back wall and raises his hand to the cabinets. He places his hand about three inches away from the surface. The cabinet slowly opens. His colleagues are stunned as evidenced by their mouths gaping open. They were looking at a 5 foot *creature* in a glass tube full of liquid.

Jonathan K. Miller

Karen says in a low tone, very slowly, "Je-sus-all-mighty-what-in-the-hell-is-that?"

Frank says, "is it human, Ethan?"

Well, I'm not trying to be a wise ass when I say this, but how in the hell would I know. It's in a glass bubble! We can't access the creature to take samples. We don't have the tools to extract the body or pieces of the body. We did come with tools, don't get me wrong, but we didn't expect to find glass bubbles! Getting back to your question, yes, we think it's humanoid. Doesn't it favor the creatures that they call the *Greys*. We looked at it through magnifying glasses and found the skin and the pigmentation liken unto a frog....we think. Looking up close, the skin cells are similar....to a frog, that is! If this being was ever alive, we think it breathed through its skin."

Twelve Blocks

Frank notices it doesn't have a sex organ. "No sex organ, he says?"

Ethan replied, "no, not that we can tell. But Frank, think about this. There are frogs that have the ability to change their sex. In a same-sex environment, there were previous studies of a frog species in the amazon forest that revealed these abilities. Maybe these beings share that capability."

Wow, Ethan!" It appears that you've identified some distinct possibilities! And you're certainly right about one thing, they do look like the Grey's, but they're green."

Ethan replies, "or the fluid turned them green."

Barry says, "Wait a minute! The *Greys* were real? There really is an area 51?"

Jonathan K. Miller

Frank says, "No, Barry, we're just saying that they look like the pictures that people described after they reported seeing the *Greys*, so calm yourself down!" Frank puts his hand to his chin, "I wonder how they got them in that tube. Look at this! You're right, no rubber seals, no nothing. A complete bubble! How in the heck did they do that?"

Unless they were transported "Ethan suggested. "They may have transported them into the tank, Frank!" The more Ethan said this, the more logical it sounded. This makes perfect sense.

Frank says, "Ethan, this isn't Star Trek, man! You are talking about a lot of "if's" here, partner!"

I know Frank, but we are not talking about anything from the planet earth. Look outside the box."

Twelve Blocks

Barry mutters, "this is something straight out of a science fiction movie or the twilight zone.....do do, do do! Do do, do do!"

Karen ignores Barry and says "this is so amazing. Are there any more?" She looks over at Ethan and repeats, "are there any more of these creatures Ethan?"

"Good question, Karen." He repeated the cabinet opening sequence and there appeared six more beings, all basically the same, but differed slightly in size and color. Two of the beings had 15-inch long arms, while the rest were more human like.

Their faces had a different color than their bodies. A lighter color with smooth skin. However, their bodies were scaled like lizards and fish from the neck down. Their bodies were completely free of hair. One of the beings had six toes on both of its feet, while another had 4 fingers, but 5 toes. All of the creatures had oversized eyes with an elongated skull and thick lips.

Karen gazed with utter astonishment and whispered, "Oh-My-God, look at this!"

Ethan said, "Now these specimens appear to be Humanoid, but with reptilian skin, like the pictures I sent to you. Barry noticed the skin looked thicker, tougher, even scalier. This was verified when he looked at the bottom of the bubble. There were loose scales resting at its bottom. The scales had turned white like snowflakes and seemed to be deteriorating from the liquid solution."

Karen says, "Do you think there is a possibility that these beings could be them Ethan? You know, the aliens, themselves?"

"Yes, they very well could be, but we don't know for sure. However, I'm thinking that they wouldn't experiment on their own kind, but again, what do we know! I'm going to throw you all a curve ball here. I just want you all to entertain this idea. What if these beings are prototypes of us. That this is what humans may evolve into in the future or rather into our future. They may have found a way to speed up genetics and study the development of mankind. But, of course, we can't be certain. Nonetheless, this very well could be how we evolved."

Frank replies, "ETHAN, you never cease to amaze me, man! That wasn't a curve ball! That was a freakin' fastball! That is a "huge" hypothesis. I like the way that you think, though! You always had an open mind. I respect that about you. How about this for a hypothetical thought! Maybe this is a "failure" of how we evolved."

Karen replies, "now that I can believe!"

Frank gets closer to the glass casing, squeezes his eyes, trying to get his pupils to focus on the beings, "You know, he says, there is no telling what we're looking at. There is not even a single, solitary bubble in the fluid. Which is another thing I would like to know! What kind of fluid is it! We have got to open up one of these suckers."

Ethan replies, "equipment is currently on the way as we speak. We found other creatures in the room next door. All of the specimens next door favor many of the animals we see today walking around."

Twelve Blocks

Barry says, "I'm going to have a bad dream about this!" Ethan's phone buzzes, and its Corporal Larry Standish from the room next door.

"Ethan says, "Yes, Dr. Collins here?"

"Dr. Collins, Dr. Wendall says she's done."

"Thanks Corporal, we'll be right there. Dr. Elizabeth Wendall is the linguist I was telling you about earlier. Let's go see what she's got."

They ascended up to level one to greet Dr. Wendall. Clothing began to reappear, and they felt heavier with a little dizziness and nausea. They began to clear their throats and rub their eyes. Doffing their lab coats they forge onward to meet Dr. Wendall.

Barry says as they are walking down the hallway,

Jonathan K. Miller

"What an experience! My mouth feels dry. I used to have really bad dreams when I was kid watching movies like Frankenstein, Dracula, and Creature from the Black Lagoon, or was that the Blue Lagoon?"

"Barry, why did I bring you?" Frank jokingly asks.

Barry replies, "after seeing all of this, I'm not totally sure that I even qualify to be here!

They reach the end of the hallway and to the right they see Dr. Wendall sitting at her laptop entering information.

Ethan says, "Elizabeth, what do you have?" Elizabeth looks up from her laptop not expecting to see anyone but Ethan. She begins to smile with twinkles in her eyes when she sees Frank," then replies,

Twelve Blocks

"Ethan, I would normally say that you are not going to believe what I just found, but we are way past the non-believing stages!"

Ethan begins to introduce his colleagues, "Elizabeth, this is..." Elizabeth cuts him off, "Dr. Frank Deneb, from the University of Chicago?"

Frank says, excuse me?"

"I was your student at Arizona State 15 years ago."

"Really?" Frank said.

"Yes, Dr." And my recollection is you told me one morning in your class that I had the "gift for gab."

"Don't tell me," Frank replied, "let me guess, you were talking when I was talking and you should have been listening, right?"

Jonathan K. Miller
"Correct. You told me I had a gift for gab, that I
needed to shut up, sit down and listen. Bring back any
memories?'

   "So you became a linguist?"

   "No, I stopped talking when you were talking, and
then decided to become a linguist." They all laughed,
and Frank replied,

   "I'm sure glad that worked out for you. Wait, wait,
wait, he said! You were that young lady with the
florescent green fingernail polish that glowed when you
entered the room every Thursday! The young lady who
questioned everything I wrote about the dynamics of
space on the time continuum in the Beta system. I also
gave you an "A" for interpreting the facts on that
archaeological find in Peru if memory serves."

"The one and only. Dr. Deneb".

"Well, I'll be. You're the only one that received an "A" in that class as I recall. You turned out to be one of my very finest students that year. How did you remotely become a linguist?"

She said, "I actually had a gift for gab." That statement brought huge laughter.

"I'll be darn," he said! He reached out to shake her hand, "Call me Frank".

Ethan said, "Elizabeth, this is Dr. Peterson and Dr. Bennet."

It's a pleasure to meet the both of you." Barry and Karen returned pleasantries asking Elizabeth to call them by their first names.

Jonathan K. Miller

Ethan said, "What have you got for us Elizabeth?"

"Well, we deciphered documents that suggest that we, as in, us humans, were considered to be property."

"Property?" Ethan replied! "Are you saying that these beings documented that they own us?"

"Yes in manner of speaking. More like documented us for a future generation. It appears to indicate dates of matureness, and times of, shall we say....harvesting the food source."

"Harvest? Did you say harvesting the food source? Ethan questions.

"Yep, harvest!" Karen replies.

"Harvesting who or what Elizabeth?" Frank jumps in.

"I don't know. It goes in the direction of

mathematics, then back to dates and times."

"Is there a chance you could be wrong about this Elizabeth. We can't be guessing about something like this. What are you suggesting?" Ethan asks.

"I'm not suggesting anything! I'm also not the only one coming up with these conclusions. Dr. Lee, Dr. Miller, Dr. Fineberg, and Dr. Hawthorne have analyzed the same equations and they suggested that the aliens were working on a nutritional supplement."

Ethen is now shaking his head and replies, "they were working on multiple projects. To suggest that we are some kind of delicacy is a bit farfetched, don't you think?"

Elizabeth said with a slight edge to her voice, "after everything that you and the rest of us have seen in this place, why would this be a preposterous thought?"

Karen comes to Elizabeth's defense and declares.

"VERY GOOD POINT Elizabeth"

Elizabeth says, "Listen, who in the world of Ba-Jesus, would want to end up inside an alien lunchbox, Ethan? I'm not making this stuff up, and you know what else? It doesn't sound so bizarre either! I'm telling you this is what we understand from these transcripts. The aliens were working on their future. Here's another (as you say) curveball for ya, Ethan. It's not far in their future!"

Ethan's eyes opened, "Whoa, whoa, whoa! These labs are millions of years old."

"As far as we can estimate, yes, they are. If you think I have a logical explanation, about this, you have another thing coming! We are seeing a pattern that suggests conversations on harvest, time, travel, even flavor and

that is fact."

Barry says, "GET OUT! Whaaaat! Can you be wrong

about this Elizabeth? I mean, even a little bit?"

"Barry, we have the very finest scientists working on

this. You guys are not the only ones looking around here

with slap-jaw-bug-eyes! When we figured out what we

think these tablets were indicating, EVERY LAST ONE OF

US tilted our heads like a confused German Shepard

hearing a high pitch sound!"

Frank said, "Lets go back to this time thing." They all

looked at him. "Does time travel appear anywhere on

the tablets as words used together?"

"Not that we can see, however, the dialogs could be

thrown into the computer and the computer can make

a stab at sequencing those particular words into a

sentence."

Ethan said, "Why haven't you already done that?"

"Come to think of it, we actually may have done that.

I believe Dr. Hawthorne was feeding the computer

sequence sentencing. I'll go and check on that. I'll be

right back."

Ethan says, "I'll be back as well, I'm going to get

something I want all of you to see. We found

monograms on level 2 that are quite interesting."

Frank says, "Barry, Karen, let's call MIT and consult

with Professor Yamato from Japan, to discuss the time

travel thing. I wonder if this lab was abandoned in the

same pattern as the deserted lab in Arizona. We may

have had a continuum shift on earth and they extracted

or something else occurred which we can't identify right

now. Maybe someone else stopped these beings in

their tracks. The other similarity is that they prepared

these labs for a return trip. They wrapped up the boxes

here, put things away and departed. They prepared

both facilities with the intent to come back. My

hypothesis is telling me the earth hiccupped on them

and that's what caused them to depart."

Karen says, "The structures on both these labs are

protected by something we don't understand, but they

didn't seem to be worried about the facility. I think it

was their safety they were concerned with, and not the

destruction of these facilities."

"Okay", says Frank, "that doesn't sound too

farfetched. A logical deduction Karen, but there are too

many unanswered questions, to make any kind of

conclusions just yet. Guessing is one thing and facts are

another. We just don't know enough yet. I want to take

a look at the text, Elizabeth is talking about."

Corporal Standish suddenly steps into the room. "Dr.

Deneb?"

"Yes Corporal."

"You have a phone call coming in at the com area.

It's the President of the United States, Sir."

Everyone's eyes open wide! Frank wishes they would

stop over reacting every time Calvin's job title is

mentioned.

"Thank you and where is the com area?"

"I'll escort you Dr. Deneb.

The com deck is on Level 2, at the end of the

hallway. The room is 13 feet high and 105 feet wide. Its

doom is shaped with consoles on two sides of the wall.

Both consoles were littered with black switches and

knobs with symbols under each control switch. It

reminded Frank of the movie "Pearl Harbor" when the

lead mechanic says " lots of switches and stuff"

Only three stool chairs occupy this room. There is

one extremely bright, square light, located in the center

of the ceiling and in the center of the floor, directly

above one another. Both lights are slowly pulsating. The

room temperature is 29 degrees, with condensation on

all the switch panels. Unlike the rest of the rooms

discovered this room is grey and smells like honey. The

floor is soft and slippery.

"Hello, this is Dr. Deneb."

"Frank, this is Calvin."

"Yes Sir?"

"Frank, we found another facility."

"Where Mr. President?"

"Mt. Elbrus, Southern Russia. It's inside the mountain at an elevation of 10,500 feet."

"Mr. President, do you happen to know the elevation of that mountain?"

"Stand by, I'll ask." Calvin places Frank on hold for what seems like an eternity. The phone clicks back on and the president says,

"18,510 feet. It was located a month ago. I'm sending telemetry to your location as we speak. I have a question for you, which is the main reason for this call.

Who would you recommend that I send to Russia to

represent the US on this project?"

Give me a minute Mr. President."

"Certainly Frank."

"Frank places his hand over the phone receiver and

says, "Corporal, may I have a moment in private?

"Yes Sir". Corporal Standish stepped out of the room

and closed the door behind him before Frank resumed

his conversation.

"Well, Sir, Dr. Peterson is here with me, and I trust

her implicitly. She is an expert in her field and can

handle herself in any given situation. I am confident

that she knows what to look for and what questions to

ask and so forth. She is also very good at documenting

her findings which is vital to any investigative or

research project. I have the utmost faith in her abilities

and trust her instincts."

"Didn't you tell me that this was her first out of the

country assignment?"

"Yes sir, I did, but she has the gift, Mr. President. She

has the character and work ethic that it will take to

work on this project. As I said before her writing skills

are outstanding and necessary to meeting the

challenges associated with this type of project. You can

see firsthand her capabilities when you see my report

tomorrow. She has the uncanny ability to ask the right

questions and present the possibilities. A solid scientist,

through and through!"

A slight pause as the president thinks...."I trust you,

Frank. Send her."

"Yes Sir. Mr. President....are the Russians cooperating with us?"

"Yes they are! As strange as it may seem, they are very cooperative. So bring me up to speed on your findings in Africa?"

"Sir, from the information we have thus gathered, we have a processing laboratory here."

"Processing?"

"That's what I'm told, Sir."

"Ok, what do they think was, being processed?"

"You want that over the phone, Mr. President?"

"This is a secure line, go ahead?"

Jonathan K. Miller

"Yes sir. I'm told they were, processing humans, but the humans look vastly different from present day humans. It appears that they were trying to create...us, Mr. President!" There was silence on the phone for several seconds.

"Creating us as in...what, Frank?"

"Mr. President, I would say, thus far, that this looks to be a human manufacturing laboratory. I must also add that there is still a lot of speculation. None of this has a shred of fact attached to it, yet. We are still very much in the guessing game. I'm sending pictures with the information to your office."

"I see." The President replied in a solemn tone of voice. "Frank, I'm sending you more help. Give me a full report by 5:00 pm tomorrow, DC time."

Twelve Blocks

"Yes Sir." The President hangs up the phone and slowly walks to one of the windows behind his desk in the oval office, and looks in the distance contemplating the news Frank just delivered. How is this possible? Could Frank and his team of scientists be right? Boy, the media is going to have a field day when they find out about this discovery, if it proves to be true. Perhaps, we should keep this from the media and avoid the frenzy the news will create. No doubt it would create chaos. Lord, help us if this proves to be true!

After Frank was finished speaking to Calvin, he found Corporal Standish waiting outside to escort him back to his colleagues. As he returned to the room where his fellow scientists were chatting, he shared the information he received from Calvin. "Ok, we have a brand a new development! The president is sending us more help. They also found another lab in Russia. Mt. Elbrus, to be exact."

"I had a feeling that you were going to come in here and announce that very thing," Barry ask, "In Mt. Elbrus or on top of Mt. Elbrus?"

"Inside the mountain, at an elevation of 10,500 feet. The mountain is 18,510 feet. That puts the facility approximately 8,010 feet, 2 million years ago, so it too was underground when it was constructed."

"That's providing it was built 2 million years ago. We certainly don't know that for sure!" replied Karen.

"Yes, this is true, Karen. I'm basing those facts on what we have found thus far. Also, Karen, the President is assigning you to head up the project."

Twelve Blocks

"ME? Me? Are you sure Frank? The President is sending me?"

"Yes, YOU."   Frank laughed as he answered her multiple questions.

"Frank, I've never...."

"You'll be fine, Karen! A jeep is on the way to pick you up."

"WHAT? Frank, I think we need to talk about this!"

Of course, we can do that. I'll brief you on what the President will need from you." Karen is clearly shocked and has mixed emotions about accepting this assignment. Just as Karen is about to ask Frank further questions, Ethan enters the room with additional news.

"I need everyone to take a look at this. These are the

tablets we found on the lower southwest deck. They were 4 levels down from us, not 3 levels. Frank, did you get your phone call?"

"Yes, they found another lab, Ethan."

"Incredible! Another one? Where is it?"

"Russia! The President didn't elaborate very much. He just stated that the Russians found it about a month ago. He also said that the Russians are cooperating fully with us. Karen is leaving tonight to spearhead the investigation."

Ethan smiled at Karen, and looked over at Frank and says, "good choice! We're going to need a strong scientist over there. Congratulations, Karen, I'm sure you will do well." Ethan's comments couldn't have come at a better time. Karen suddenly felt very proud of herself and the fear melted away. With her self-confidence somewhat restored she began to think that maybe, just maybe, I can handle this. Hey, why not, I made it this far. This will be good for me. She began to smile and inwardly thanked Ethan. Outwardly, she stated, "Thanks Ethan. I appreciate your vote of confidence."

"Frank," says Ethan, "what did they find inside the Russian lab?"

I don't know yet Ethan. The President is sending us more information." Frank stopped to take a look at the tablets Ethan brought into the room. "Ethan, it appears that the symbols on these tablets are identical to the ones on the tablets we found at the Arizona site. Look at this. I downloaded these pictures on my laptop. They are the very same, except for this symbol at the bottom.

Other than that, they are identical." Did Elizabeth's team view these yet?"

"Not Yet." replied Ethan.

"What level is she on?"

"She's two down.

"Corporal Standish, would you go find her?"

"Yes sir," Corporal Standish left the room immediately to find Dr. Wendall. About 15 minutes later, Larry returned with her in tow.

"Elizabeth, would you please take a look at this." requested Frank. "These symbols are identical to the symbols in Arizona except for the bottom pattern. Will you give these tablets to your team to examine and report the findings to me."

Twelve Blocks

"Sure, oh wait a minute...we have seen these symbols all over the facility. It appears to be a memo or a message sent throughout this facility. The symbols on the bottom seem to be numbers; a date or a time. Look at this one? It says the same thing, but the bottom has a different symbol and then it changes on this block. This is a message pattern. Not to change the subject, but Ethan, you have to see the console in the next room. There are some switches in front of what looks to be a viewing screen. My staff are about to switch it on."

"What?" says Frank! "Who gave them the authorization to do that? No one has the authority to activate the systems. We better get over there pronto." Having said that, Frank, Ethan, Karen and Elizabeth run into the next room and Ethan shouts: **"WAIT, WAIT!",** but it's too late. The switch has been activated.

Jonathan K. Miller

Chapter Six

First Contact

They hear a humming sound as soon as the switch is activated. Everyone is standing there waiting for the world to blow up! The hum becomes louder and the room begins to vibrate ever so slightly. The temperature is becoming increasingly warmer. The walls are turning a light shade of green and the lights in the ceiling are getting brighter by the moment. All of a sudden, a high pitched whistle which sounds like it's coming from the ceiling begins to drown out the humming. Frank notices the video screen on the console getting brighter.

Twelve Blocks

Frank says, "The screen just activated! Looks like an empty room! It too, was the color of green. All eyes are glued to the monitor as the form of a body begins to take shape on the screen. "Oh my goodness, says Frank!"

The clarity of the body is improving and the frame is thin, brown, with almond shaped eyes, bald head and hairless. No ears are detectable, and it looks to have small holes on each side of its head where the ears should be. The arms are thin, the torso is small, and its fingers are as long as the neck. There is no nose, but two holes where the nose should be. It stood in front of a console, similar to the one in the room the scientists occupied. Its height appeared to be approximately 5 foot 5 inches tall, if the room console is the same height. As it was materializing on the screen, it

Jonathan K. Miller

remained transparent.

Karen says, "what the heck is that", in a voice so low,

that you could barely hear her.

Barry replied, "I know what it's NOT! It's not human,

that's for sure!"

"Oh my God! Should we turn the switch off?"

Elizabeth asked.

"No, not yet! Let it take shape! We seem to have

activated some sort of transport system. Let it

materialize." Frank said in disbelief as he watched the

apparition appear before his eyes!

"Well, it's here Frank!"

"Indeed, it is Karen! Ok, let's turn off the switches!"

David Hatcher, an Intern Technician for Dr. Wendall

flipped the switches that he initially activated.

Everyone in the room was frozen as David clicked the switches off. The hum began to whine down, the lights dimmed, and the room turned to its original light gray.

Frank says, "Would you look at that? Are there any armed soldiers on site Ethan?"

Before Ethan can respond, Corporal Standish responded without hesitation. "Yes Sir!

"Well don't you think we ought to get them down here on the double?

Yes Sir, right away.

"It looks confused." Elizabeth observes.

"Yes and disoriented. And I would be, too, if someone snatched me away from where ever I came from. I believe it's looking right at us." All eyes turn to

the being and silently agree with Frank.

Barry is the first to comment, "It sure in the hell is

and it's moving toward the screen!"

The being begins to operate the console and the hum

begins to escalate in the room occupied by the being,

although not as loud and the pitch was slightly

different. The room began to mildly shake.

Barry says, "The hum is back."

"Yes, we hear it, Barry. I think it just activated its

console!" replied Frank.

"NO SHIT!' David said.

Barry said "It's pointing at us?! It's pointing at us!"

"I think it's trying to tell us something Frank."

Twelve Blocks

"Yes, it appears that way Ethan, but what the hell is it trying to tell us?"

"I believe it wants us to turn the switch back on!" Karen suggested.

David says, "O-o-o-o-k, um, what should we do folks? Things like this don't happen in Nebraska."

"Alright Ethan, you're the lead here, what do you want to do?" Asks Frank.

"First, where are those damn soldiers? Larry arrives five minutes later rushing into the room.

"Sorry it took so long! Personnel were spread out on several Levels and communications were down. All personnel are now stationed right outside the door sir." They almost felt sorry for Larry.

He was clearly out of breath and sweating from the exertion of searching on each Level.

"It's pointing again," says Barry!

"Barry, PLEASE." says, Frank, "stop with the blow by blow commentary, we can all see what the thing is doing!"

Elizabeth says, "It definitely wants us to activate our switch!"

David says, "Hey guys, the thing seems to be agitated! What should I do Sir? Oh Shit! It just spit...something!"

"I think it's in pain, Turn on the switch, David." Ethan says.

"Yes Sir." David flips the switches and nods his head

so everyone will know the switch is back on. Seconds

begin to pass. 5 seconds, 10 seconds, 15 seconds.

Barry is the first to say, "Well?"

"Wait a minute," said Frank! "It's adjusting

something on it's console."

Karen says, "It's turning on a bunch of switches!"

The hum is growing louder, the lights are getting

brighter and the facility begins to vibrate, but not mildly

this time. The team is thrown off balance, grabbing the

console and one another to keep from falling down. As

the vibration continues, two more beings begin to

materialize on the screen. They look identical to the first

being.

David says, "We have two more, Sir! Two more of

those things have just beamed in!"

Elizabeth moved closer to the viewing screen "Oh, my goodness."

Barry says, "Ok, now we have three of these things looking at us! The humming sounds begins to whine down.

David turns around to Ethan…."It's powering down the system, Sir. I believe it wants us to turn off our switches. Should I do it?"

"Yes David. Shut it down."

David reaches over the console and turns off the switches as directed. "I'm done!

Barry then asks, "What's going on? They'er talking, but we can't hear what they're saying"

Twelve Blocks

"How many soldiers do we have here, Larry?" Frank asks.

"25 Sir."

"Any officers?"

"Yes Sir."

"Do any of them speak English?"

"Yes Sir. Major Cendowi just arrived at the facility, and he speaks English fluently."

"Good! Ask Major Cendowi to join us."

"Yes Sir." Larry left the room and headed for the stairs to the upper Level where he last saw the Major. Unable to find the Major, Larry asked the soldiers stationed on this level if they might know where he could find the Major. One of the soldiers said he heard

Cendowi state that he was going topside for some air.

Larry rushed to the elevator and began the ascent to

the top and the exit. He found the Major focused on

the Valley below. As he approached, the Major signed

heavily and said, "I fear that our country may see much

turmoil if we cannot find a solution to our violent ways.

I wish to see my children grow to be strong men and

women. I want to grow old with my wife and spend

time with my precious grandchild. This is all that I wish

for? How can I help you Corporal?"

Ten minutes later they entered the room to join the

scientists. Good afternoon everyone. I am Major

Cendowi. The Corporal indicated that you requested

someone who speaks English fluently. I can

accommodate your request".

"Hello Major. Thank you for joining us. I'm sure you

and your men experienced the shaking that occurred a

short while ago. We activated several switches on the

console and managed to teleport what appears to be

some form of living beings to this facility."

"Excuse me", says the Major.

"We have visitors, Major!"   Ethan turned to the

monitor and stepped back so the Major could clearly

see the screen.

"In the name of Timba, what the hell are they?" the

Major rhetorically exclaimed.

Ethan stated, "It's almost like they have visitors. They

don't seem to be interested in leaving their room."

"You know, you're right," says Frank! "Why is that?

They also appear to be very calm."

Major Cendowi asks, "Is someone going to explain to me why we have alien beings in here?"

Ethan says, "Elizabeth, can you take the Major over to the side and fill in all the details? Elizabeth nodded her head and she and the Major move to the side of the room out of earshot.

Frank says, "what room are they in? Do any of you recognize the room?"

David quickly responds, "We don't know Sir! I think they are lower than we have ever been, but we can't identify the exact location."

"By the way, who are you and who gave you the authority to activate switches?" Frank says clearly agitated.

Twelve Blocks

Barry interrupts Frank, "They're pointing at us again! I think they're trying to tell us something about the console. Whoa, whoa, what did it just do?"

It's changing the camera angle on the console. I believe it's pointing at the 5th button. It wants us to push the 5th button." David says excitedly.

Ethan said, "What camera David?

"I'm assuming they have a camera. They touched something and the picture changed to the switches on their console. I think he's showing us what switches to activate."

Ethan said, "Okay, go ahead and push it David."

The Major suddenly interjects, "Wait! Don't touch that button!"

"Major," says Ethan, "I think it's trying to

communicate with us."

"Thank you Elizabeth for bringing me up to date."

The major walks over to the console where everyone is

standing and says, "Yes, well you don't know that, do

you? You push that button and all of us could wind up

as dust on the floor or be vaporized. Not a chance that I

am willing to take ladies and gentlemen."

Barry says, "Spoken like a true military soldier!"

The Major continues, "We don't have a clue who or

what these things are and you are ready to invite them

to dinner. They don't seem to be in a rush to go

anywhere. I suggest that we just sit tight and observe

them for a while. In the meantime, we're going to get us

some backup firepower and make ready to protect

ourselves."

Ethan replies, "While I appreciate your concern Major, I would like to remind you that I'm in charge of the operation at this facility. As a scientist it is my duty to expand our knowledge and gather the facts which are derived from direct observation and study. This may involve taking unnecessary risk, and I am willing to take this chance. We have already pushed buttons and we're all still standing here."

"No, Ethan,"You were in charge here! I'm taking over now that we have a potential threat to my country. As of this second, this project is now a military operation, under Ethiopian jurisdiction. You will not be pushing any buttons without authorization of the President of this nation. Please remember, that all of you are guests in our country!"

Jonathan K. Miller

"I knew this was coming sooner or later," muttered Karen under her breath.

Major, I do have permission to conduct this operation under your president's authorization, Ethan said defensively. "I suggest YOU stand down." The major walked to the door and in a loud voice called for Sgt. Pabuto. He then turned and walked over to Ethan and positioned himself within 10 inches of Ethan's face as Sgt. Pabuto entered the room.

"Sgt. Pabuto," the Major declared in a loud voice! "Yes Sir!" "Sgt, you will set up a perimeter in this room and at every entrance on this level. As of right now, no one is to communicating with those beings, operate any machinery, or enter into any rooms without my direct permission. Is that clear Sgt?"

"Yes Sir," And furthermore, if anyone disobeys that

order, you will shoot them, is that clear Sgt?"

"Yes Sir, very clear Sir!"

"Do you now understand me Ethan? I will not allow

you to endanger the lives of these people for your own

personal curiosity or scientific pursuits. I do understand

your commitments and your responsibilities and I

greatly admire these attributes. However, you did not

have the authority to bring those "beings" here. Once I

establish contact with my superiors and update them

on this "latest development", the decision will be that

of the President to continue this operation. Is that clear,

Doctor?"

"Ethan took a deep breath just as Frank walked over

and whispered to him not to challenge the Major. In a

calm voice Ethan replied in an aggressive tone.

"Major, you're barking does not intimidate me. I am not one of your soldiers, and I do not have to take orders from you. Is that clear? I need to speak with your president, Major. You are way above your pay grade here. We have the archaeological find of the century, and I do indeed, have total authorization from your president to conduct this operation."

Frank can't help but wonder what has gotten into Ethan. We are in a foreign country and rely on the African military to protect us. And let's not forget that we are visitors. Ethan needs to rein in his emotions before none of us make it home safely.

The major responds with a voice that is focused and unwaivering, "Then you will have nothing to worry about when I contact the President's office. We will

find out soon enough just how much authorization you

hold in OUR country. Dr. Collins, you will remain here in

this room with your team until further notice and rest

assured that you will be shot should you disobey these

orders. The Sgt. has his orders. I suggest that you and

your team not challenge these orders. You-will-be-

killed!"

   To make the point even clearer, the Sgt. ordered

twenty soldiers to enter the room and station

themselves around the perimeter. They carried deadly

assault rifles with enough ammo to kill a herd of

elephants. They were then instructed by the Sgt to pull

back their rifle chambers readying for action. Karen

glanced outside the room into the hallway and

observed another 30 or so soldiers with assault

weapons.

"Everyone else must leave until further notice. I'm sorry it had to come to this, Doctor. You have your job and I have mine. Sgt, carry out my orders!"

"Yes Sir!"

Meanwhile, the beings stared motionless observing the activities transpiring in front of them. Frank walked over to the Corporal and instructed him to contact the President of the United States and explain as best he could the latest dilemma. With military aplomb, Larry asks the Sgt. if he can leave the room to contact the President of the United States. The Sgt. respectively grants permission to the Corporal.

"Barry, isn't the Sgt. the stinky guy?" Karen whispered in Barry's ear.

Twelve Blocks

"The Corporal returned about 15 minutes later and hands Frank a note. Frank closes his eyes, says a silent prayer, and shakes his head after reading it...Shit, Shit, Shit! When it freakin' rains, it pours, he whispers out loud to himself. Frank lifts his shoulders and shakes his head at Larry to see if the President is on the line. Larry shakes his head, no. Then Frank walks over to Karen and Barry and hands Barry the note. It reads, From the United States of America. The President's office has assigned General Braxton to your location. He will arrive at your location at 0900 hours tomorrow to assist you and your team to assist or negotiate a resolution to the situation.

"Why does Calvin persist on sending General Braxton. He knows how I feel about the General."

"I see the God's do not favor us again," says Barry!

"Dr. Deneb, phone call for you, Sir."

Finally, Frank whispers to himself. "Thank you Corporal."   Frank puts his ear to the phone and says "Hello, yes, Mr. President, there has been a new development!" Frank commenced explaining to the president everything that had transpired over the last 30 minutes and to get further instructions. To Frank's surprise, the president said there was nothing he could do about the decision making at this point. However, he did say that from this point on, Frank and his team were to be advisors only to Ethan, as well as Ethan's team and the officials of Africa. They were not, under any circumstances, to make final decisions, but to advise only, unless they were in grave, physical danger. Protect your team at all cost, stated the president.

Frank hung up the phone and walked over to Sgt.

Twelve Blocks

Pabuto and says, "Look at us, Sgt. We are a bunch of scientists. Do we even remotely look dangerous to you? We are just specimen testing, test tube filling, microscope viewing nerds, given an assignment of the millennium. We are not criminals. We are not Dr. Frankenstein or even Igor, and we certainly are not going to challenge you, or your soldiers holding those deadly weapons at our heads. We wouldn't even challenge your soldiers if they didn't have a single rifle! I humbly request that you instruct your soldiers to lower their weapons, please? They look somewhat nervous and we don't want any accidents resulting in loss of life."

Sgt. Pabuto acknowledged his concerns and gave the order for his soldiers to lower their weapons.

"Thank you, Sgt. Pabuto, thank you very much."

Twenty-five minutes passed by. The beings never moved. Everyone jumped when the phone rang on the Corporal's hip.

"Dr. Denab, it's the president again, Sir."

Frank takes the phone and says, "Hello Mr. President, this is Frank."

Frank, the Ethiopian government did contact my office. The African President has dispatched a representative from his office to make any decisions. He will arrive any minute now. Remember, you are not to make any decisions from here on out. You and your team are now advisors and observers of the United States."

"Advisors. Yes sir."

" I've instructed Larry to keep an open line, and we will monitor by audio, as it unfolds.

"Very well, Sir. Thank you Sir." Frank hands the phone back to Larry and nods his head to say, he understands the open communication with the president.

Major Cendowi returned a short while later and walked over to Ethan, "Dr. Collins you have been authorized, once again, to lead this project in consultation with a representative from the president's office. The president is sending someone momentarily. When he arrives, he will conduct operations with you. Until he arrives, you are in control."

Thank you Major," says Ethan. "Do you think we could remove a few of your soldiers from the room? It's overly crowded and a bit unnerving for us civilians."

The major agreed and ordered Sgt. Pabuto to handle the request.

As the soldiers exit the room, Elizabeth says, "I'm going to click on the switch to see what they are trying to say. David, will you monitor the controls?"

"Yes ma'am."

"Okay, here we go" and she flips the switch. Everyone holds their breath waiting for some kind of adverse reaction. Three seconds, five seconds, and then it's up to 25 seconds and nothing has happened. No shaking, no humming, pure silence until….

"Kalebra," says one of the beings!

"Who was that," says Barry? "Was that one of them

who spoke?"

Frank puts his four finger to his mouth to signal him not to comment, then says, "yes, that was one of them!"

Elizabeth says, "It's, I mean, they are adjusting the video camera"

The being once again repeated, "Kalebra."

"Ok, Ethan, talk back," replies Frank!

Ethan says, "Hello, can you hear us? Do you understand us?"

"Yes, we understand you," replied one of the beings.

"Who are you," says Ethan?

We do not have a verbal name for our species. It is a

sound. If we verbalize our name, it would damage the delicate skin you call an eardrum. We are from another world, in another galaxy, existing on your planet in another dimension. We have come to your planet many of your earth years ago."

"Please allow me to introduce myself and my colleagues. I am Dr. Ethan Collins. To my right, is Dr. Frank DeNeb, and Drs. Karen Peterson, Dr. Barry Bennett, and Dr. Elizabeth Wendall.

"May I ask, why did you come to our world?"

"To develop life on the planet."

"So you are telling us," says Ethan, "there was no life on this planet when you arrived?"

"In a manner of speaking, yes. No life as you know

it," "All the elements were here, but life as you know it was not developed."

Ethan says, "We would like to come to your location to greet you."

"Please do not do that. Your atmosphere is not compatible to ours. Our immune system as well as yours will be contaminated. However, we can provide instructions on how to adjust the atmosphere from you station which would enable you to come to our location.

Ethan says, "Stand by, please." He motions for Elizabeth to click off the audio switch. "What do you think, Frank? I don't sense any threat or danger to us."

"I agree with you about not feeling a threat, however, this is a time where you have to expect the unexpected.

Jonathan K. Miller

I can't make the call on this one, Ethan."

"I understand and that's sound advice. Ok, Major, do you feel any threat with this next request, or is it time to get a higher authority in on this."

"I think that we should, indeed, get an official diplomat in here. We are not trained negotiators Dr. Collins."

Agreed. Let's wait for the representative to arrive."

Frank says, "Do you know how to turn off the console viewing screen, Elizabeth?"

"David you switched this on, and I don't know the sequences."

The Major says, "Ok, let's wait for the time being. We must wait for our diplomat to arrive before pressing forward.

Barry said, "Wait, are you kidding?" Frank rolls his eyes at Barry and tells him to shut up. Karen smiles and shakes her head.

The Major says, "Very well, Mr. David, you may switch on the audio sound," however, if you ask me, I think we need to speak to our diplomat before we continue further communications. Don't you agree?"

Frank, Ethan, Elizabeth, and Karen all nodded in agreement.

"Is there anything we can do to make you more comfortable," the Major asked of the beings.

"No, we have all we need for now."

The Major continues with another question, "Can you

turn down the humming sound from your console? It's

starting to affect our ability to balance ourselves and we

are becoming disoriented."

"No, we can't do that without losing the essence of

our dimensional form. Our suggestion would be to

relocate to a higher level."

"Is there a way to view and speak with you from

another level," says Ethan?

"Yes, Level 1 and Level 2 will resolve the problem.

We recommend Level 2. That Level generates a higher

energy flow. The room at the end of the hall has a

console identical to the one in front of you. We can give

you directions from there."

Ethan said, "we didn't see a room at the end of

those two halls."

Twelve Blocks

"You must step up to the wall to activate its doors. The wall will respond to your movement and provide you access." The immediate thought in Ethan's mind was all the rooms they must have passed right on by in the course of exploration inside the facility. He realized they had and have no clue as to what they have found.

"No Shit," says Barry! Frank thinks to himself, he's hopeless, the man is absolutely hopeless.

Ethan says, "Stand by, please. He knods at David to once again cut off the audio. "What do you think, Frank, Level 2?"

"Well, according to them, yes. It's there facility. They know the power source a whole lot better than we do."

"Okay, Level 2 it is. Alright everyone, we need to keep someone down here until we can establish viewing and sound contact from above. We turn this thing off and there is no telling what can or will happen. Frank and I will stay. Major, everyone else can go."

Ethan says: "Elizabeth, we may need your expertise top side on Level 1. If something happens to us down on Level 2, you will have to make the decisions."

She nods her head, "I understand."

The Major calls Sgt. Pabuto on his cell phone. "Sgt., I want you to form a team of ten to watch this station, but keep your weapons out of site. I don't want them to think they have been imprisoned. Set up a com system on Levels 1 and 2, and a secured, com system on level 1 that would tie into the President's office. Use the rest to set up a perimeter at the front door. Under no circumstances can anyone enter this facility without authorization. Doctors, are you sure you are going to be all right here?"

"We'll be fine, Major," replied Ethan.

"Very well. Let's go." The officers leave the room. Ethan decides to make small talk while everyone is transitioning to new positions. He realizes he didn't introduce himself properly so he asked David to turn on the audio switch.

"Hello, My name is Dr. Collins. We have some questions we would like to ask you. Is this ok?"

"Yes, you may Dr. Collins."

"We found two other facilities on the planet. Did you build them?"

"Yes, and twelve others.

Frank replies, "twelve others?"

"Yes, Dr. Deneb"

Frank couldn't resist, "What are the functions of these facilities?"

"There are many functions. Developing life on your world was our prime directive. The balance of our atmosphere, gravitational fields, dimensional vortex, velocity and many other aspects are the main functions to sustain us."

"Each facility has a different function?" Frank asks.

"No. They all serve the same purpose."

Ethan says, "Did we cause the three of you to enter into our dimension by accident?"

"Yes. We were aware that your species would figure

out how to activate the system."

"Were you a part of this particular facility?"

"We are a part of all the facilities on your planet."

"Are you the leader of your people," says Ethan?

"No. We have no leader."

Frank says, "How do you get around to all of your facilities?"

"Your dimension is a single entity, our dimension is not. We have the ability to be in more than one place at a time."

Elizabeth says, "and just how do you accomplish that?"

"There is no time in our dimension as you know time.

Jonathan K. Miller

We shift in space, not in time. All who have been chosen were chosen by the collective. All of us helped to build all the facilities on this planet and other planets in one way or another. You identify builders as engineers. Our builders make the choice who will help construct."

Frank asks, "The facility you constructed in our desert on the American continent, it's more like an earth city to us because of its tremendous size. How many of your species lived there?"

"All of us lived there. We are still occupying all facilities on earth, but in a different dimension."

"You left many items in our dimension when you departed. Why did you leave these items?" asked Karen.

Twelve Blocks

"We left them for you."

Barry says, "Can you see us? I mean, while you are there, working in your dimension, can you view us as you work?"

"We can. When we need to and when we want to." The doctors felt a sense of creepiness sweep over them at this response. It's one thing to know that you are being watched by someone nearby, but totally different in knowing that you are being watched by an unseen entity.

Karen says, "Where is your home world?"

"Many galaxies away. Your world has become our world. We occupy the same universe. Our space is in between your space."

Frank says, "Why did you build your facilities in our dimension if you live in another dimension?"

"To help you exist, to help you to evolve and grow, as well as to help us exist."

"Exist to do what," Frank ask?

"To Live."

Frank says. "Ethan, hold on. Excuse us for one moment, please." Frank motions for David to turn off the audio. "Something is not right, Ethan. Did you hear that? They built these facilities to help themselves. We obviously can't help them. He's answering all of our questions without caution, so I don't feel like we are in any kind of immediate danger."

"Do I hear a but, Frank?"

"I don't know. Doesn't it feel a little awkward to you?"

"Ethan shakes his head with a slight nod indicating "no".

"Ok, let's continue to ask them more questions. David flip the switch again, please."

" Do each of you have names, Ethan said? The beings suddenly appeared to be frozen. There was no movement and no sound emanating from them. "Excuse me, do each of you have names? Is something wrong? David, is the audio working?"

"Yes, it is doctor."

"Why in the world are they staring at us like that?" A rhetorical question at best.

Karen eventually says, "Ethan, they are motionless.

They simply aren't moving!"

Hey Doc, what the hell, they're becoming

transparent. You can see right through the things."
David

said with some anxiety in his voice.

Karen says, "Oh my goodness, would you look at

that!"

Someone shouted. "Their eyes, look at their eyes,

they're following our movement."

Ethan says, "Hello! Excuse me? Hello? Can you hear

us? What's going on?"

Frank says, "I think they're phasing in and out of our

dimension!"

"Yeah, I think you're right! They're in our dimension, and probably theirs too! Extraordinary!"

Finally one of the beings responded to the question, "Yes, each of us has names.

"Whoa! Talk about a delayed reaction," says Barry.

"Do you have any questions for us? Ethan asked"

"No, Dr. Collins, we have no questions."

"Do you mind if we ask a few more questions,"

"Please continue," said the being.

"When you phased into our dimension," says Frank, "you needed our help to bring your colleagues. Why? Why did you need our help?"

"The power levels in your dimension are weak. After

so many of your earth years, the particle beam needs to

be recharged. Our dimension holds power without

weakening. Your console gave us additional power to

breach the dimensional doorway into your dimension

with the console in the compartment you occupy."

"What else can we do at our console," says Ethan?

"We will show you."

"Hold on," says Frank! "Ethan, we will get to that

soon."

"It's alright Frank. I just want to see where he's going

with this."

"The console before you has a split level dimensional

arc, which gives the console the ability to tap into the

universal energy flow of this galaxy, distributed by

Twelve Blocks

surrounding stars. The console we operate has the ability to hold the energy stream in a balanced form to allow travel between dimensions. Both consoles must be activated simultaneously to keep the energy flow from being interrupted by additional portals being used at the same moment. The portal in the room you occupy identifies the signature flow from this console and allows the dimensional portal to stay activated. That is why we asked you to switch on the console to allow the others of my species to join me in this dimension."

" I see. Why were you in the portal beam line?"

"I...we were traveling at the moment you activated your console. Because the console in this room was not activated, the particle beam power line was weak. The streamline was interrupted bringing me here."

"Why was it so weak," says Karen?

"Because the three of us were traveling at the same moment, within the same arc line. We needed more power for the three of us to jump into your dimension."

Karen asks, "Where were you traveling from and where were you traveling to?"

"We have a facility located inside what is currently called Mt. Shasta, on the continent that you call the United States. We were being transferred in particles to a facility under your Mediterranean Sea."

"Oh my God," says Karen!

Ethan says, "Why did you construct so many facilities in our dimension? Why not build them in your dimension?"

Twelve Blocks

"It was needed to fulfill our goal of creating your life."

"Our life", says Karen? "You created humans?"

"Yes, we did Dr. Peterson."

"Frank, look", says, Ethan! "They're phasing again. They're transparent! Hey! Hey, can you hear me?"

Karen says, "there has to be a reason why they are continuing to stay in a transit stage. Let's ask them when they phase back."

"They said they needed our console to be active." David interjected.

Frank replied "It is active, so the signal can't be weak. The color of their skin changed when they phased this time, did you notice?"

"Yes, I did," says Ethan, "It looks like they're coming back. Can you hear us? Hello, can you hear us?"

"Yes Doctor, we can hear you."

Ethan asks, "Why are you continuing to stay in a transit mode?"

Frankly doctor, your species does not instill trust in one another, and therefore, we have the same reservations. Your actions have recently demonstrated that you may do harm to us while we are in your dimension. We must be able to protect ourselves and depart this dimension quickly if a threat is imminent."

"We understand your concerns, but we are not here to harm you. We are merely here to observe and report our findings to our leaders. The facilities and your presence on our earth is a great discovery that could alter our beliefs of how we came to be. Might I ask if

there are any others of your species aware that you are

with us?"

"Yes."

Barry says, "Are they watching us right now?"

There's that creepy feeling once again.

"Yes, Dr. Bennett."

Corporal Standish steps into the room and says, "Dr.

Deneb, you have a call from top side, and I also just

received word that the Major is on his way back down

with a representative from the President's office."

"Excellent. Um, which president's office Larry?"

"The Ethiopian President, Sir. The Major's ETA is 10

minutes."

Jonathan K. Miller

"Hello, this is Dr. Deneb."

"Frank, this is Kyle Jorgenson". We have the data from the computer, and you're not going to believe what the computer is telling us."

"Oh, but I would, go ahead, Kyle."

"The tablet reads, we are complete and then the number on the bottom of the tablet indicates a vast amount of something that the computer can't decipher. Now for the part you won't like. It appears they shut down the system after receiving this tab."

"Why wouldn't I like that?"

'We think they shut down, according to the tab last week."

"Last week! That's impossible!"

Twelve Blocks
"Yeah, well, the computer says it's not!"

"How can that be Kyle? This place is the oldest thing

we have ever uncovered. Kyle, the place is millions of

years old! Maybe the computers are out of sync!"

"Out of sync? Frank, what do you want me to tell

you?! This is what we are getting from the

computers, man! All the facilities received this

information, and then they all shut down *last week*,

according to the computer's analysis."

"Alright, Kyle, thank you."

"Yep."

<u>Chapter Seven</u>

"Dr. Collins, you have a call coming in, Sir." Corporal Standish announced.

"This is Dr. Collins.

"Dr. Collins, this is Ambassador Gehunwa, from the President's office. I apologize for the delay. Both the Major and I have arrived. I will be there in five to ten minutes. And the Major is on his way down as we speak. Do we know what they want from us?"

"We don't know just yet, sir. We're trying to find that out now"

Twelve Blocks

"I quite understand under the circumstances! I have to make a phone call first and then I will head your way for a debriefing."

"Very well sir."

As they look up Major Cendowi walks into the room.

"Hello, Major, welcome back," says Ethan.

"Hello, Dr. Collins. What's the status?"

"We found out some very interesting information."

"Well, we are eager to hear what you have to report.

"Major, we are going up to the second level to establish communications." Says Ethan.

"Why the second level?"

"The power efficiency is much stronger on Level 2

according to the Beings." We have located the room

that the beings so graciously informed us about and

have prepared the room for contact.

"I need to get word to the Ambassador that we are

going to assemble on the second Level." The Major

grabs his walkie talkie and proceeds to call Sgt. Pabuto

asking him to inform Ambassador Gehunwa to report to

the second level.

"Dr. Collins, can you inform the beings that we are

ready and are transferring operations to Level 2", the

Major requested.

"Yes, I can."

"Okay," Let's proceed." Ethan signals the tech to turn

on the audio and everyone starts moving out.

Twelve Blocks

Ethan says to be beings, "we are transferring to the room you suggested. It will take about 10 minutes for everything to be in place." The entity responded that they understood, and indicated that they would re-establish contact in ten minutes. Ethan nods his head for David to cut communications.

As they head for Level 2, Ethan brings the Major up to date on the latest information. The ambassador completes his phone call and heads down topside with his assistant. Frank briefs Karen and Barry on the President's instructions. Everyone emerges in the room at approximately the same time.

As the door opens, they are all surprised to see a room 15 times the size of the room they just vacated, along with a viewing screen 10 times bigger on two cables above the east wall. Cabinet compartments, machines and devices totally foreign to anything they have ever seen occupy the room. They also see 8 foot long glass tubes that are empty and suspended from the ceiling on a vine like rope about 10 feet above their heads. The ceiling is around 40 feet high. There were seven, 9 foot archways, 5 feet wide leading to other rooms.

The console on the west side of the wall was identical to the lower room, with the same number of switches, knobs and buttons. There is a single light in the center of the ceiling and a light in the center of the floor directly above one another. The light on the floor is flush. The light in the ceiling is a bubble. The ceiling light pulsated as if controlled by a generator. The beings had once again, told the truth, however, this room was much more like a laboratory built for tall residents.

Twelve Blocks

Ethan directed the staff to their positions just as

Ambassador Gehunwa and his assistant entered the

room.

Are we ready to contact the beings, Dr. Collins?"

"Yes, Major, we are ready?"

Before we get started, I'd like to introduce,

Ambassador Gehunwa, from the Ethiopian

administrative office of the President."

"Hello, everyone," It's a pleasure to meet everyone."

One by one each of the doctors began to introduce

themselves to the Ambassador. He walked around the

room and shook everyone's hand. He was rather soft

spoken and warm hearted with a very pleasant

demeanor. He was liked immediately by all whom he

approached, which was every single person in the room.

Jonathan K. Miller
A small man, with soft hands, and a big heart.

When he finished meeting the scientists he said, "I'm told, that our visitors are willing to show us how to make the atmosphere in their room compatible for both of our people to communicate face-to- face without contaminating one other. Are we ready to move forward?" Every person in the room nodded in agreement. He then said, "let's get started."

Ethan motioned for David to turn on the console. The console reacted immediately and the screen activated as expected. The beings appeared on the screen. The reception on the screen was crystal clear.

Gehunwa asked, "Can they hear us?"

"No, the com is turned off." says Ethan.

Twelve Blocks

Okay, explain how we are supposed to fix the air Dr. Collins."

More like dimensions, sir."

"More like dimensions, what does this mean, more like dimensions?"

"The console in their room must be in sync with the console in this room. They told us that a series of switches in this room is needed to activate whatever it is in their dimensional realm. Doing so will merge our two dimensions. Did I explain that correctly, Frank? Barry?" Both agreed with his explanation. "We decided that we didn't want to greet them face-to-face without someone official from your President's office."

"Wait, wait, wait," he said! "I understand the representation aspects. Let's go back to DIMENSIONS!"

I'm afraid you lost me. I am not a scientist so you will need to explain this to me in layman's terms."

"Oh, yes, well...this could take a while. The beings are in a different dimension than ours, Sir. They cannot interact with us in our dimension and vice versa, until we fix the space between our two dimensions to accommodate both our species. In doing so, they have volunteered to give us instructions on how this can be done using both the console in the room they occupy and the console in this room."

"I see! replied the Ambassador. "This is more serious than I thought. So, this is not an atmosphere problem at all! It's a dimensional space problem? And here I thought they didn't want to catch a cold!" Everyone smiled at this soft spoken, warm hearted, charming man!

Ethan, says "No, Sir, it's both, actually. It's the face-to-face contact as well as the atmosphere. This is why we wanted you here to make the first physical contact."

"I see, and I am honored to be included as a representative of the President of Ethiopia."

"There is something else, Ambassador" says Ethan. "While you were traveling here, we have been asking them questions As we conversed, they started phasing in and out."

"What? Please do explain further."

"We call it "phasing" when they move back and forth from their dimension to our dimension."

"But I thought they were in their own dimension already and needed our help to get into ours?"

Jonathan K. Miller

"No sir, they need our help to combine the two dimensions together so that we can occupy the same space without contaminating both dimensions." The Ambassador shook his head in a confused way.

"Ambassador, they are in their own dimension, phasing in and out of our dimension, using a transistor particle beam. They are prepared to depart in an emergency, using this floating phasing procedure, if needed. The process only takes a few seconds, but while it's happening, while they are in flux, the line of communication is blocked. We asked them why they are continuing to stay in flux and they replied...We can't be trusted. Our species can't be trusted."

"I see. Alright, then...well they don't trust us and that makes us even, doesn't it?"

"I suppose it does, Sir." Ethan conceded.

"Is there anyone else in this room that thinks they can't be trusted, or, that we should NOT enter into that room? This would also mean, should we "NOT" be hitting any switches at their command? Major, I'll start with you?"

"I really don't know sir," says the Major. "So far they have not demonstrated or given us any indication of hostility. As far as we can see, they have no weapons or defense protocols in place. For me to say that they are dangerous at this point, well, I don't have a cause to do so...yet."

Ethan, how do you feel?"

"I'm willing to give it a shot. I'm a scientist, sir. I would like to know more about them and if this is the way to accomplish that, I vote we do it."

"I suppose you feel the same way, Dr. Deneb?"

"Sir, they haven't demonstrated any hostility, I agree with the Major on that. As an observer from the United States, I am instructed to do just that, observe. I can't inform you on what you should or should not do. That being said, I will say as a scientist, the need to know more about a new species is overwhelmingly addictive.

"We seem to have all the right people in play here with the proper authority to move forward."

The president is listening on the open line on the Corporal's phone and is very proud of his friend and the choice he made to send his friend to Africa.

"Very well," says Ambassador Gehunwa. "Dr.

Wendall, your opinion, please?"

"I have mixed feelings, sir."

"What do you mean Dr.?"

"I want to trust them, I really do, but... But?"

"But what,"

" I'm skeptical"

"Skeptical about trusting them? Why?" The
Ambassador presses.

"I suppose I just don't know enough about them. As
a scientist, I have an obligation to research, observe,
question and document my findings. But I'm not usually
faced with coming into contact with a being from
another planet, dimension, or whatever you want to call
it that could have been my creator. It's an unsettling

feeling for me."

"Hmmm, for the record Dr. Wendall, I'm going to take that as a "no" from you. Can one of you tell me how you would judge their personalities thus far? From what I have already heard, they appear to be a non-aggressive species."

Ethan volunteers and says, "They have been very polite, very calm, extremely direct, answering all of the questions we have asked of them. They don't seem to be hiding or dancing around any questions. Except for telling us what their names are, but with an explanation that by doing so it would hurt us. There is just no way, at this point, to tell if they are lying to us or not. In all truth, I think they are trustworthy."

"I see. Do you all agree with that?" The group

nodded in the affirmative. "What about you, Dr.

Wendall...do you agree with their demeanor?"

" Yes, I do Ambassador."

"Okay then. Although Dr. Wendall has reservations

about making contact, I think we need to show a leap of

faith and continue our communication with the beings.

Mr. President, are you with us?"

The President of Ethiopia speaks over a loudspeaker

intercom system that only a choice few knew was

connected. "Yes, I agree with you Ambassador

Gehunwa. Please continue." Everyone raised their

eyebrows with surprise! Frank looks over at the

Corporal who nods his head that Calvin Sinclair, the

President of the United States is in agreement.

"Yes Sir, thank you Mr. President." Dr. Gehunwa

Jonathan K. Miller
looked around the room and said, "Ladies and

gentlemen, a leap of faith is what we are about to do

here. However, we do need to take some precautions,

just in case Dr. Wendall is right." He looks over at

Elizabeth and smiles. "We have always wondered if we

were alone in the universe. We search and we search

and thus far have not been able to find a single entity in

the vastness of the universe. Today, it appears that all

of those questions and more are about to be answered.

We did not go to the universe today. The universe has

come to us."

"Let us go forth, as Dr, Deneb has wisely said earlier

and explore our possibilities. Working together, all of

us, we will represent our race. The human race, as one!

But let us do so wisely." It is an honor and a privilege to

be a part of the history we are making today. It is

time."

The Ambassador looks at the major, speaking directly to him. "We will lock the facility down, Major, nobody in or out. Contact your forces and have them on standby to obliterate this site at any sign of hostility. I want someone's finger on the button! Tell your soldiers to pull back to a safe zone. Give me a separate phone line to the President on that phone over there in the corner."

Major you, Dr. Wendall, Dr. Collins and please forgive me for not remembering your names will stay with me to greet our visitors face-to-face.

"Do I need to know anything else at this juncture, Dr. Collins?"

"Yes sir," says Ethan, "the Beings have informed us

that there are 12 facilities around the globe and all of them are currently occupied by the Beings, but in a different dimensional context."

"So what you are telling me is that none of their people are in our dimension?"

"Not that we are aware of Ambassador. Just the three we know about, but they are traveling to and from all the facilities around the globe, just (again) not in our dimension."

"I can't begin to tell you how confusing this all sounds, but I think I do understand all that I need to know for now. Anything else?"

Frank says, "Yes, sir. We think you should know, that the three of them were in flux, or rather traveling to another facility in their dimension, when we accidently interrupted their flow. That is how we discovered their

existence. We don't remember the sequence of how we

did it, but they are going to show us, according to

them."

"I think I've heard enough. Let's do this, folks. You

must be the technician? What is your name?"

"David, sir."

"Let's open the channels David.

"Hello, my name is...FOR THE LOVE OF TUMBA,

WHAT IS HAPPENING IN THERE?"

"This is the phasing we were telling you about." says

Frank.

"My goodness gracious, you can see right through

them!" The Ambassador exclaimed.

"Give it a few seconds, they'll come back." Ethan

explained.

"Amazing! Absolutely incredible! Their skin

is...is...orange?!

"Yes, then they turn back to green-ish, blue-kind-da-

sort-a."

"Kalebra", replies one of the beings.

"Ambassador," says David. "It's talking to you Sir."

"Oh! HELLO, MY NAME IS AMBASSADOR

GEHUNWA!"

Frank says, "Sir, you don't have to yell."

"I beg your pardon?

"You don't have to yell sir. They can hear you in a

normal tone of voice."

"Thank you Dr. I better start over. Hello, my name is Ambassador Gehunwa. I represent the President of the Ethiopian government. I am told you would like to interact with us. And the atmospheric conditions must be altered to sustain for you and us alike. Is this true?"

"Yes, you are correct."

"I have also been informed that you will provide us with instructions on how to accomplish this?"

"That is correct Ambassador."

"Very good, very well. So what would you like us to do?"

"You must go to the third panel".

The third panel is over there, Ambassador, Elizabeth

Jonathan K. Miller

directed.

"Thank you, Elizabeth."

"There are twenty eight switches on the bottom panel and 32 control knobs on the top. There are 14 buttons under the knob switches."

"Yes we see them." Elizabeth replied.

The Being then directed them to the last switch on the right as the first switch to be activated followed by the first two switches on the far left with the far left switch being activated first.

Elizabeth responded, Okay, what's next?"

The final instruction was to go to the far right again and turn the first knob to the left. Elizabeth followed the directions exactly.

Twelve Blocks

Karen whispers to herself, "What's happening?"

One of the Beings states that the system is now activating the environmental control unit and there is nothing to fear.

"The floor is beginning to vibrate! Is this normal?" Asks theAmbassador.

" The system is activating the safety shield around the facility. It is normal, do not be alarmed about the vibrating, replied the entity."

"We can't hear you very well. Is it normal for the floor to vibrate?"

"Yes, it is normal Ambassador."

Elizabeth says. "Ok, what's next?"

"The center switch is next,"

Jonathan K. Miller

David is unsure and looks to Ethan for help. "Is this the control switch they want me to flip on?"

"No, I believe he means the switch to the right of that one."

" This one, here?" asks David of the Beings.

"Correct. "You must now wait for 3 of your minutes before activating the four switches on the far right." The minutes tick by very slowly. The tension in the room is palpable.

Frank is apprehensive about their decision, and excited as the same time. What a discovery!

What an opportunity! The world as we know it is about to change. For better or worse!

Elizabeth replies, "Ok, three minutes have passed."

Twelve Blocks

Ethan says, "Go ahead and click them on, Elizabeth."

Elizabeth flips the four switches on the far right as directed. The walls begin to turn red.

"What is happening to the facility?! The walls are turning red!" Frank says.

The beings reply, "The system is rejuvenating its energy."

Elizabeth, says, "Should I continue, Ethan?"

"I don't know. Did we do anything incorrectly?"

Again, the Beings reply "No, all is as it should be."

Elizabeth replies, Ok, now what? She is then asked to turn on the four switches below the other four switches simultaneously.

"I would assume these are the four?" asks Eizabeth.

"Yes Dr. Wendall, you are correct."

Elizabeth then flips the switch and a surge of electricity shoots up her arm. In an instant, her brain capacity increases 67% and she yells, "OH, MY GOD!"

Corporal Standish says, "Sir, top side reports are coming in that facilities around the world have been activated!"

Major Cendowi says, "Activated how? What do you mean?"

"Sir, apparently we turned all of them on! All the facilities have been turned on, Sir! The whole Earth is shaking!"

The Ambassador says excitedly, "What's going on!? Please tell us what you have done!"

Twelve Blocks

"Sir, the laboratories are rising from the ground! We're moving, WE'RE MOVING, SIR!" Shouts the Corporal.

Ambassador Gehunwa replies, "What did you do!? TELL US, WHAT YOU DID?"

The beings reply, "It is the period of "Cleasah". The time has come for our species to replenish ourselves. We have given your species time to multiply your numbers and develop into matureness. This stage of the process is now complete. Our facilities have been activated to process your planet. Once our facilities reach the surface, it will take approximately nine of your days to cycle the earth and two of your months to prepare and stock our storage facilities. Our supplies are depleted. Please do not resist us. All of your defensive capabilities have been rendered inoperative.

Processing of your species has already begun. It is a

painless procedure. Do not fear, none of your species

will suffer any pain. You will simply...go to sleep."

   "Oh my, God, we opened the gates!" Karen

screeched with unbridled fear in her voice.

   The Major yells out, **"WHAT ARE YOUR ORDERS, MR.**

PRESIDENT?" The President trys to respond, "Detro..."

as communications are interrupted.

   A monsterous voice erupts from one of the Beings.

"The time has come for harvesting the human crop on

planet Earth."

   The earth begins to shake violently, and a low hum

begins as the facilities worldwide continue to rise up

out of the earth. The lights begin to dim, all the doors

slam shut. A high pitch whine joins the hum like the

sound of a jet engine winding up. It begins to

increasingly get louder. There is absolutely nothing that

anyone can do.

There is a loud popping sound and the door slides

open, then closes again. One of the soldiers standing

near Frank panics at the loud sound and accidently fires

his rifle. The bullet ricochets off of two walls and strikes

Barry in the head. He drops. Karen screams. Frank runs

over to Barry.

Jonathan K. Miller

Chapter Eight

The Awakening

Sgt. Tomba Pabuto suddenly walks through the west wall and passes through the room and heads to the east wall. He pulls a stone out of his pocket and holds the stone up close to the wall. The stone begins to glow a soft green. The wall creates a socket and Pabuto sets the stone into the socket. The stone turns a vivid blue.

Then Pabuto opens his mouth and a searing, incredibly loud screech comes from his mouth. Everyone grabs their ears and collapses onto the floor, knocked out cold. Their ears begin to bleed. Everything electrical around the globe shuts down, except for all

twelve facilities planted around the world. Outside of

the facility, planes are dropping out of the sky,

manufacturing plants are shutting down. Satellites

orbiting the earth begin to veer off course and collide

with one another plunging to earth or drifting out into

space.

The screeching voice of Pabuto suddenly stops. He

walks through the wall and into the room where the

Beings are standing. For the first time, the Beings

exhibit fear at the sight of Pabuto. They open their

mouths as if to scream, but nothing comes out. Pabuto

closes his eyes, and the Beings vanish into oblivion in a

matter of seconds.

He walks back through the wall and into the room

with the contingent of doctors and officials. He closes

his eyes and opens his mouth. The high pitch screech begins to come forth once again, but it is at a different pitch level. The whining noise begins to soften. The ground stops shaking. The screeching from Pabuto's mouth stops. You can still hear explosions from all around the world from aircraft hitting the earth. 90 minutes pass and everyone begins to slowly wake. Pabuto has returned to the room where the entities were standing looking at the console monitor screen. David sees him first.

David is the first to speak. "Look, Sgt...Pabuto is in the next room. Where are the Beings? They're gone." Pabuto is standing with his eyes closed.

The Ambassador groggily asks. "Who is Pabuto?" Everyone is now awake and standing, but shaken from the incident. Frank, however, is kneeling beside Barry.

Twelve Blocks

He takes his pulse…..nothing! Frank curses himself for

being so hard on Barry.   Karen sensing how Frank feels,

joins him and places her hand on his shoulder. He looks

into her eyes and hopes his appreciation for her

concern is recognized.

She squeezes his shoulder and gives him a moment to

collect himself. She found a white lab coat and gave it

to Frank to drape over Barry's body. The room was

silent, everyone lost in their own thoughts.

In response to the Ambassador, Frank says, "I have

no idea, but I'm sure we're about to find out."

As all eyes are on Pabuto, he begins to fade away and

reappear in the room where everyone is standing. They

move out of the way and give him a wide birth.

"The Major is the first to ask, "who are you, can you

tell us what just happened?"

Pabuto opened his eyes ever so slowly. His eyes were glowing a bright green. He opened his mouth and a voice like a speaker spews forth. Every human on the planet could hear his voice in all languages known to man.

"We are the Cyclomons. Please do not be alarmed. I have been sent to your planet as an emissary to watch over the species who created you. Your creators are called **"Porthia"**. The Porthia" have been on this planet from the time your solar system began to form. My species, the Cyclomons placed the Porthia on this planet because they were criminals in our galaxy. Earth was to be their prison."

"Millions of your earth years ago, our system was

Twelve Blocks

attacked by the Porthia. We defeated them on our planet and eventually destroyed their world. At the point of annihilation, we decided not to destroy all of them. Their planet was devastated. We collected who was left of their race, and brought them to this solar system. Your solar system did not pose a threat to any species nearby so the decision was made to place them here on your world. We were not without compassion. We gave them the tools to produce their own food so they would not parish, but took away their ability to reproduce. Your species was created by the Porthia as a food and service source. As they harvested and recreated more humans, your speicies began to evolve into what they are today. There have been many harvest periods. Each period left signs of their existence. Your period of evolution was the greatest.

We began to see intelligence in human beings beyond what the Porthia could speculate. There have been times when we recognized unique or superior intelligence and we removed some of your species to other solar systems. The Mayans, Niya, Angkor, Nabta, Turquoise, Indus, Cahokia, and many others. We placed them on worlds that have allowed them to live out their lives in peace with the ability to reproduce and advance their culture."

"The Porthia have the ability to move through your bodies and influence you to behave according to their needs. You call them spirits. Your race has been writing about them for many of your earth years. Unfortunately, you do not have the ability to understand the thoughts transmitted through your consciousness as provided by the Porthia. The true essence of the identity of the Porthia are energies of

consciousness with the ability to take solid shape. They

can only take solid shape when it is time to nourish

their energy.

"It is my race that built the facilities on your planet.

These facilities are called Comkeys. There are twelve

comkey blocks of Porthia. Each comkey possesses their

own population. They will live out their lives in

approximately 7 million of your earth years, then they

will parrish. There is a protective beam that surrounds

the planet that prohibited the Porthia from departing. It

will be removed when we extract them. Your

gravitational field around your planet will decrease by

1.37 1/4%.

"We gave the Porthia the ability to travel from one

facility to another in a form unfamiliar to you. The

facilities were strategically located to allow the Porthia

to use 97% of the planet to travel. The connection of

the Porthia is the basis of your spiritual thinking. The

first facility was located at the area

you called, The Garden of Eden. Your beliefs started at

this point. Your twelve tribes, for example, your twelve

disciples, your twelve numerals on your time clock, your

twelve hours of night and day are all influenced by the

Porthia."

"Your species could not comprehend how you were

being produced so you created your own....God. This is

how we have come to the conclusion that you deserve

to evolve on your own. Your history shows many Gods

that you felt you needed to create. You demonstrated

the need to feel superior over those with less

intelligence. You have demonstrated the ability to care

for one another. The Porthia did not give you this

ability. You developed this ability on your own. Now

that you have been made aware of your origin, you may

begin again with what you call....the truth."

""You are now human beings with a path to become

whatever you evolve to be. It has been decided by my

race to give your species a chance to further evolve. The

Porthia were raising your species like cattle to harvest

you for food. You have been granted this opportunity

from my world to continue living because you have

demonstrated the ability to achieve a higher

intelligence level that may be useful to your universe in

your future."

"You will notice that your bodies will feel different

from this day forward without having the Porthia inside

of you. Your species will be connected closer to one

another with the telepathic ability to see and feel each other's thoughts. It will take some time to adjust, but you will evolve. Your brain will now have the ability to operate 100 percent of its capacity. This will help you in your telepathic adjustments...in time. This ability will not give your species a way to hide from one another any longer. This is necessary for your evolutionary progress. Our species will monitor your progress. As you evolve, you will begin to see...your universe, your life, your being."

"We will give you four of your earth hours to vacate all Porthia facilities. The removal of the Porthia is now complete. We will remove the comkey blocks from your world and place them on the Porthia's new world. Those humans who are still inside the comkeys when the extraction is complete will parrish. We beseech you

Twelve Blocks

to remove all of your kind from the comkeys. Please do

not remove any items from the comkeys, for all items

will also be removed in the transformation. Your earth

is now yours to do what you will. A representitive of our

world will arrive in 7 of your earth days. At that time we

will begin to monitor your progress and assist your

species with the assimilation into the universe. We wish

you well."

Pabuta began to disappear, and he reminds them

once again before fully disappearing, "Remember, you

have four hours to vacate the blocks."

As everyone watches Pabuto slowly fade away

before their eyes Frank says...

"Thank goodness there is always a bigger fish in the

sea."

Jonathan K. Miller

Ethan says, "Well, there goes the Jesus Christ theory, now what are they going to do?"

Elizabeth, says, "I really, really, really, really, really, really want to go home!"

Major Cendowi says, "This is going to be a very interesting report!"

Ambassador Gehunwa says, "this will change all the history books!"

Karen says, "Thank goodness for the stinky guy!"

Both Presidents are thinking, "I have lost my power."

And everybody heard both Presidents thoughts loud and clear.

Karen gives Frank a long hard stare. In her thoughts she says, I would assume it is impossible to keep Frank

Twelve Blocks

from knowing he is Joey's Father now. Frank's head
whips around toward Karen, speaking in a low whisper,
he says, "What!? He heard every thought that came
forth from her. His eyes were the size of silver dollars.
Karen noticed that everyone was now looking in her
direction. They all heard her thoughts as well! She puts
her hand over her mouth as if she had spoke out loud.
Information begins pouring into all of their minds at a
rate according to they're hereditary gene pool.

A new Bible begins now...

EPILOGUE

Notations by Dr. Frank Deneb

(Archeologist) Ithaca, New York

*T*he age old questions that the human race has

been asking from the time of the beginning has

never been answered. Our scholars, theologians

and scientists can only hypothesize the answers

with our limited abilities. These questions were not

answered because we have not found any other

beings or entities that were here before us to give us the insight of the crucial questions. No one has been able to tell us **"WHO"** we are, **"WHY"** we were created, **"WHEN"** we were created, **"WHAT"** is the purpose of our existence, and **"WHERE"** did we come from, "UNTIL NOW".

We reference "The Holy Bible" and countless other bibles. We are told by many generations before us that God influenced its contents, but written by the hand of man and translated into dozens of different languages throughout the world. The books that have been written in our history informing us of our existence are about to be thrown out.

Jonathan K. Miller

The five questions above are about to be answered. The human race will experience a metamorphasis. A revelation into our true existence. Discover who God truly is. What God wants mankind to do. How to serve the master. We will find out our complete capabilities and full potentials. From the beginning of mankind to our new beginning of being able to use 100% of our brain capacity. the human race will now be able to advance and turn ourselves into a power that reaches far into the universe, without leaving the very ground we were created from. The ability has always been there for our species to advance, however; the opportunity was held back, by God itself.

Twelve Blocks

The moment has come for humans to be more

than what we are and without limitations placed

upon us. Time as we measure it with our devices,

are about to cease and a new era will begin. A new

world without laws and regulations. The human

race is about to find out that such directives are

simply not necessary. Man will also find out that

there is, indeed; a fountain of youth located inside

the human brain and we will live forever.

.

TIME, has run out...

DEDICATION

This book is dedicated to my wife who put up with all long hours of being ingnored. All the times that I made us late for dinner meetings and other functions because I just had to write the ideas coming forth for this book. I also dedicate this book to our dogs, Holly, Poopie, and Saffra, who were very patient on the days when feeding time came much later than it should have.

ACKNOWLEDGMENTS

This is my first science fiction book that I have written. It would not have come to pass if it wern't for my editor and wife, Jacqueline Miller. When I Informed her that I was thinking about writing a science fiction book, she immediately encouraged me to start because of my love for day dreaming. It was then that I asked her if she was insulting me on which she replied, No, with a smile. She later came back to me on that same day and said that she was, indeed, serious about me writing my story and offered her help to assist me. I felt so good about that, that I dove in to the project. She was there as she promised every day to deliver hot tea or coffee, dinner or lunch at my desk, and even completed a fair share of my ranch duties when the animals started looking at us funny because their dinner was late...again! Jacqui was good on her promise and I want the world to know that I appreciate all of her help. Thank you, Jacqui for being that silver lining.

Twelve Blocks

Written by Jonathan K. Miller

July 19 2016

Made in United States
Orlando, FL
29 January 2022

14186913R10188